Praise for *Jawbone*

"This bodily, propulsive narrative re-envisions mainstays of the Latin American novel for a 21st-century feminist sensibility based in Internet creepypastas, true crime, and women's autonomy. Expertly characterizing her protagonists while providing an engrossing, compelling story, Mónica Ojeda has hewn out her own version of contemporary gothic set in Ecuadorian culture. Sarah Booker's fluid translation admirably attends to the book's many complicated voices, situations, and registers."
—**Judges' Citation, 2022 National Book Award in Translated Literature**

"Strange, twisted . . . . Ojeda, who was named one of Granta's best young Spanish-language novelists, writes with a polyphonic verve, agilely translated by Booker. Her language, like adolescence itself, is unruly and excessive, full of dramatic shifts and capable of both beauty and horror."
—**Anderson Tepper**, *The New York Times*

"*Jawbone* depicts the process of becoming a woman as the ultimate horror story. . . . With terrifying ease, Ojeda illustrates how womanhood is characterized by dualities: fearful and feared, desired and desiring."
—**Morgan Graham**, *Chicago Review of Books*

"Rife with gothic body horror and the darkness of the jungle and within ourselves. . . . Ojeda is a strikingly singular voice, combining basic teen angst with stark madness and the power of teen girls to push back in a world that tries to make them powerless." —**Yvonne C. Garrett**, *The Brooklyn Rail*

"Delectable. . . . There are echoes of Lovecraft and Shirley Jackson at play, but the vision is ultimately Ojeda's own—delicious in how it seduces and disturbs the reader as the girls rely on horror both as entertainment and as a way of staving off the actual terrors of growing up. This is creepy good fun." —***Publishers Weekly***

"Edgar Allan Poe meets a few of the mean girls. . . . Mother-daughter relationships slide under Ojeda's microscope, sharing space with the teacher-student dynamic and deities as objects in an exploration of power and sexuality during adolescence. . . . Every good horror story needs a victim; Ojeda's monsters and victims wear the same faces." —*Kirkus*

"*Jawbone* distinguishes itself through fevered brilliance. . . . Like the strange bloom of a corpse flower, the novel evokes life, death, and a vortex of twisted beauty." —**Meg Nola, *Foreword Reviews*, starred review**

"The horror exists in, and is generated by, a delicious but unsettling uncertainty of self and non-self whereupon realities are created and cast off. . . . Ojeda's poetic craft shines through *Jawbone*'s prose. It's a deeply visual book in which seemingly transparent images introduced early on are lacquered over with layers of meaning as the story progresses, building a patina of dread." —**Annabella Farmer, *Santa Fe Reporter***

"Dark academy meets existential horror in this scintillating and unsettling novel of friendship, adolescence, and 'inquietude.' When a group of friends find an abandoned building, their most charismatic member slowly escalates their afternoons of scary stories and dares into a secret society of dangerous rituals and potentially deadly consequences. The characters are entrancing, the ideas are insightful, and the prose itself is thrilling." —**Josh Cook, Porter Square Books**

"Mónica Ojeda is fearless in her approach to both themes and style. She deals with horror and desire like few others, with a beauty so extreme that it sometimes leaves you gasping. In *Jawbone,* an elite Catholic school becomes the stage for nightmares fueled by obsession, creepypastas, and teenagers crazed by hormones and horror movies. But in the end, the novel is about Mónica's primary concerns: sexuality, violence, and how a story about the damaged and the lost can be told with such beauty and relentlessness. She scares me, and she amazes me, and I think she is one of the most important writers working in Spanish today." —**Mariana Enríquez**

"Mónica Ojeda has at her disposal the most enviable combination I can imagine, and she has it in spades: a lucid mind, an exacting language, and a wild heart." —**Andrés Barba**

Nefando

Nefando

Mónica Ojeda

Translated by Sarah Booker

COFFEE HOUSE PRESS

Minneapolis

2023

First English-language edition published 2023
Copyright © 2016 by Mónica Ojeda
Translation rights arranged by Agencia Literaria CBQ SL
info@agencialiterariacbq.com
All rights reserved
Translation © 2023 by Sarah Booker
Cover design by Kyle G. Hunter
Book design by Rachel Holscher
Author photograph © Lisbeth Salas

First published by Candaya as *Nefando,* © 2016

Coffee House Press books are available to the trade through our primary distributor, Consortium Book Sales & Distribution, cbsd.com or (800) 283-3572. For personal orders, catalogs, or other information, write to info@coffeehousepress.org.

Coffee House Press is a nonprofit literary publishing house. Support from private foundations, corporate giving programs, government programs, and generous individuals helps make the publication of our books possible. We gratefully acknowledge their support in detail in the back of this book.

LIBRARY OF CONGRESS CATALOGING-IN-PUBLICATION DATA

Names: Ojeda, Mónica, 1988– author. | Booker, Sarah, translator.
Title: Nefando / Mónica Ojeda ; translated by Sarah Booker.
Other titles: Nefando. English
Description: Minneapolis : Coffee House Press, 2023. |
Identifiers: LCCN 2023014947 (print) | LCCN 2023014948 (ebook) |
    ISBN 9781566896894 (paperback) | ISBN 9781566896900 (epub)
Subjects: LCGFT: Science fiction. | Horror fiction. | Novels.
Classification: LCC PQ8220.425.J433 N3413 2023 (print) |
    LCC PQ8220.425.J433 (ebook) | DDC 863/.7—dc23/eng/20230331
LC record available at https://lccn.loc.gov/2023014947
LC ebook record available at https://lccn.loc.gov/2023014948

Translation of quotation from *The Butcher* © 1991 by David Watson. Original text © 1988 by Alina Reyes.

Fly illustration © Sammy Bennett. Used with permission.

Cover images: chick embryo © OnyxRain / iStock.com; crocodile skin © kynny / iStock.com; Optical Coherence Tomography (OCT) © Best_Shop / iStock.com; perspective squares © teamplayfor / iStock.com.

PRINTED IN THE UNITED STATES OF AMERICA

30 29 28 27 26 25 24 23   1 2 3 4 5 6 7 8

If I sit down to think
the apple is stripped.

AMANDA BERENGUER

Nefando

Kiki Ortega, age 23. FONCA scholar.

Room #1

It had to be She, a She, with eyes like two big, sinister, ripe pechiches, with nails like seashells and the tongue of a mollusk, a tongue like an octopus tentacle, chin-length black hair, dark black, five foot five, no, five foot four, how much do fourteen-year-old girls weigh? she wondered as she leaned back against the wall's wrinkled skin. To write means renaming the space around you, describing it as if it were something else. For example, when she wrote, she liked to picture herself surrounded by ramparts, which wasn't the same as picturing herself surrounded by drywall—that was the inappropriate, imagination-flouting word. Few things were as important as finding the right word; *no, those kinds of words don't exist, only the expressive ones do, she remembered, chewing her nails.* Reformulation: few things were as important as finding the expressive word. The wall expressed her reality: a stomach full of fingernails, pica, cannibalism. The wall behind her, therefore, was a wall, not drywall. The four ramparts of her room protected her from the language of the others; there, inside, unlike any other place, she could fashion herself by forming lines, long sentences to snort. *She had to be a peephole, a tiny hole through which the desire to desire would enter; dark, perverse, much more of a crater than Them.* The four ramparts made it possible to break syntax, the word order that always alters the product, to create her own landscapes, to paint with a boy's voice. *They would be marionettes by choice; the eyes that would peer out of the tiny hole.* Sometimes, when she wrote, greenish flakes would sprinkle onto her hair, the skin of a reptile-wall peeling off from the humidity and covering the bed and floor with chips of dried paint. *There isn't a standard height for fourteen-year-old girls; they aren't copies of one another, she thought; height doesn't matter, it isn't proportional to age.* She brushed her hand over her head like a feather duster. *They would be fourteen too. Her name would be Nella. They'd be Diego and Eduardo.*

The blank page on the screen, though virtual and imaginary, was as tangible and destructive as any other. *The blank page doesn't actually exist, she thought.* That nominal emptiness could exist nowhere but in her imagination. *Diego would be pale as the night. Eduardo would have freckles.* How hard could it be to write a novel? Reformulation: How hard could it be to write about the sexuality of three children? *A novel about cruelty, a novel meant to disturb.* Something like *The Confusions of Young Törless* but mixed with *Story of the Eye.* To disturb means throwing a stone into a smooth pond. *They'd be students at a boarding school, and She'd be the new girl.* To disturb means sleeping next to someone with your eyes open. *At first, Diego and Eduardo would be the corrupters, the stone in the pond, the eyelids open while sleeping.* To disturb means staring at a stranger without blinking until your eyes burn with tears. *The reader would have to unravel the characters and then see horror in Nella.* To disturb means scratching the paint so that sounds of life outside could be heard in the next room over. *She would be the spider.* To disturb means writing with half your body submerged in a swamp. *They, the flies.*

There wasn't even the slightest breeze outside. *Nella would read the Marquis de Sade and, like Kochan from* Confessions of a Mask, *She'd understand physical love through pain and death.* The tree looming through the window—the same one that filled with black birds pecking at the panes in the mornings—stood still and gave the impression of not existing, being only an image, a representation. A photograph on a postcard. *Nella would like torturing little animals in her amorous rituals.* She opened a can of Coca-Cola, set the laptop aside, jumped off the bed, and stepped on the wall's sloughed skin with her bare feet. *A teacher would catch Her driving needles into a kitten trapped in a plastic bag.* She walked over the organic material toward the window and peered through the branches. *That's why She would have been expelled from her previous school; that's why they'd have sent Her to Diego and Eduardo's boarding school.* She thought Barcelona was a shithole, just like Mexico City. *Filth everywhere,* she thought, and a bubbling black drop slid down her lip. *The boarding school would be strict, and it would demand obedience and discipline.* The street was called Indústria, and the same old man was pissing on the same tire of the same red Renault. *Nella would feel lost in that world of moderation.* The women walked as if their legs hurt; the summer compelled them to wear floral dresses that made their bodies into crude gardens overgrown with weeds. *Nella and the asphyxiation of the rules.* She could feel dried flakes trapped between her toes. *Nella and good behavior.* The glass was an insect cemetery adorned with splatters of pigeon shit. *Nella and her desires condemned to the electric chair.* That's how the world revealed itself to her inside; but there, surrounded by ramparts, the filth did too. *She, the spider, would struggle to understand a morality beyond her individuality.* Where there'd once been the greenish skin of the wall, there was now grayish meat, the true face of walls. *Nella would still find a way to secretly satisfy herself.* Gray was the color of stones, sharks, and clouds just before it rains. *In hiding, She would find Them.*

Scratching her head, she wondered when she'd last cleaned her sanctum, but she couldn't remember. *Everything would be written in first person.* She squinted against the scent of sweat and humidity. *Everything would be written from Nella's perspective.* That evening she would have to clean, get rid of her own waste strewn across the floor. *No: writing only from her perspective wouldn't work.* Among the shreds of reptile-wall skin were invisible pieces of her own skin, long black hairs, fingernail clippings that hadn't made it to her stomach. *The novel should also be told in their voices.* She looked at the floor like someone looking into a mirror. *We're falling apart every day,* she thought, *time erodes us, that's why you have to deceive the reader.* She'd better start writing now while the characters still burned inside her, while she was still able to sweep up her own remains. *The reader couldn't know the truth.* To write in Mexico or Spain was absurd, pointless. *You could only deceive the reader temporarily.* She didn't fully know what it was she wanted to say, but she wrote to find out; she said it was a pornographic novel about three children in a boarding school just to disguise the pressing need to speculate, to think, so the world wouldn't say she was wasting her time. *They and their cynical voices would block out Nella's true nature for a few pages.* Thinking was an invisible activity that had to be made physical somehow. *Diego and Eduardo would seem like the corrupters.* Writing was the only way she knew to sculpt ideas. *But the one with the spider's web would be Nella.* She wrote so the words wouldn't speak for her, so the language behind the ramparts wouldn't destroy her. *Diego's and Eduardo's voices are essential.* With metaphors, perhaps, she could save herself from the unfamiliar constructs. *They would be the flies.* All she wanted was to say it in her own language. *The bugs that fall into a spider's web aren't innocent.* All she wanted was to articulate herself. *My characters will be the real and I a fiction.*

She'd felt dreamt up before, when she was little and her parents took her to the circus for the first time. *The backlit room is a basement.* The actors were dressed and made up like caricatures of themselves, and their costumes didn't fit. *The room: an intestine.* Some were stuffed into them, their skin marked and red where the clothing stopped, and others struggled, with the help of thick, colorful laces, to keep the outfits on. *The room: a toothless mouth.* That day an acrobat in blue stockings fell from the tightrope, and to the audience's horror, his leg bone ripped through his skin and stockings to splash the floor with crimson. *The room: a lizard's tail.* Two muscly men carried him away and immediately brought in the elephants. *The room: a fortress.* The people forgot about the acrobat. *The room: a clearing.* The tent filled with applause and sad-eyed elephants. *The room: a placenta.* She knew, looking out at the crowd, that she was the only one who wouldn't forget the acrobat. *The room: a blank page.* She knew she was the only one who wouldn't let the elephants distract her from the fallen man. *The room: a twisted tongue.* "The show must go on" really was a terrifying motto. *The room: a stage.* "The show must go on" was the formula through which people looked straight ahead, smiling, while someone bled out next to them. *The room: a self-portrait.* That was her first contact with the indifference of the rest of the world. *The room: a cell.* She understood it better when, years later, her father left home for a woman with graying hair; before leaving forever, he told her he loved her. *The room: a wound.* At the time she knew it wasn't true but that it was part of the script dictating what a father should say to his daughter before abandoning her. *The room: an aleph.* She was revolted—because it was in the script of what a daughter should say to her father before he abandons her—when she responded that she loved him too and theatrically begged him not to go. *The room: never a room.* In fact, she remembered, she didn't really care if her father left and, if she were being honest with herself, she loved him less than Chicho—a devil-eyed Doberman that died when he was hit by a sanctified van stamped with the Virgen de Guadalupe—but she told herself that she should love him, she should be sad, this was exactly how the show must go on. *Her roomneveraroom.* She was too young to understand that departing from the script wasn't an act of perversion. *Her room: a luminous cave.* Later, grown up, everything was clearer and more complicated.

The light filtering into the room was tenuous, pallid, like the glow of a lava lamp. As with the circus, her room had a different kind of light, one that made her skin look like a disguise. *Nella, the spider, would be a character cloaked in a thick mist.* Many years ago, in the stands of a traveling circus, she fell in love with a juggler from Beijing. *Diego and Eduardo would have known each other for a long time, and They'd be together like brothers, like lovers, like friends with the minds of twins.* To write meant juggling with words. *The boarding school would be big, with vast gardens, a forest, and a lake for good children, children like the ones in Musil's novel.* She only saw the juggler from Beijing once, but she remembered his long arms made for embracing and his hands moving through the air to diligently catch all kinds of colorful objects. *At first, They wouldn't be interested in Nella, the new girl.* Were there circuses in Barcelona? *But She would catch Them doing something forbidden.* Anyway, she didn't want to go to the circus; that's what the street was for. *And They'd torment Her for catching*

Them. That's what the six-room apartment was for. *Then, involuntarily, They'd step into the mist.*

She slid her hand across the wall, feeling the rough reliefs of the shredded paint that made her think of a crocodile's spine, and knew this was the only way she could write a novel: surrounded by scales. *Even though They were only fourteen, Diego and Eduardo would be sexually active.* The smell of moisture in the room was sweet, like a platter of ripe fruit; it penetrated her nostrils and cloyed her throat. *Before Nella came to the boarding school, They would have already had their first sexual experiences with girls from higher grades.* She lifted her tongue and slid it like a snail across the roof of her mouth. *They would have also explored physical pleasure with each other.* In Mexico, writing had felt like walking on needles. *Diego and Eduardo would fall in love as intensely as They desired the opposite sex.* It's impossible to write at home, she once told her mother, as long as it's full of your shit. *They would approach the girls in the boarding school like a two-headed serpent.* Barcelona was also full of shit, but other people's shit, shit that had nothing to do with her. *Diego and Eduardo would be a single person.* That was the advantage of living in Spain: she could write as a Mexican. *Diego would have oil-slicked hair.* Writing like a Mexican meant being a waterfall without a river. *Eduardo would have the eyes of a vulture.* She was never so aware of her Mexicanness as when she arrived in Barcelona. *Diego's eyes would look beyond things.* The chauvinist motto of the UNAM, "The spirit shall speak for my race," had never made so much sense. *Eduardo's hair would cover a centimeter of his forehead with blond curls.* In Barcelona, she could write without having to prove who she was. *Vasconcelos was a fucking moron.* Abroad, few things were as true as the fact that she was. *And also an asshole.*

She walked back to the bed and flopped down next to the blank document. *The circus was a dead metaphor.* Last week she'd erased every line she'd submitted in her FONCA application. *The circus was childhood.* Twenty scrawny pages, a .docx file of languid sentences in a voice that wasn't hers, landed remorselessly in the trash can. *She wanted to start from zero.* "Remorse" was a curious word. *She wanted to write as if zero were more than a hollow.* It meant continuously gnawing at your own conscience, sinking your teeth into it like a piece of gum. *She wanted to write as if zero were a starting point.* The circus was an ouroboros devouring its own tail. *But writing from zero is impossible.* A novel could be an ouroboros. *Why a pornographic novel? Why Nella? Why Diego? Why Eduardo?* It had to be possible to create a language that didn't devour itself. Her intention, the most honest of all, was to explore the most unsettling things; to say what cannot be said. *Is there anything more human than desires and fears and the indifference to the desires and fears of others?* In the forbidden was the full creative beginning. *Literature can't be distracted by elephants, it has to set them aside and look at the fallen acrobat, take an interest in his suffering, in his grimace of pain as he's carried offstage, because it's inappropriate, disrupts the harmony, makes the spectacle obscene.* Social syntax cowered inside the forbidden. *Writing only makes sense, she repeated, if it looks beyond the elephants.* And yet the room was still a reptile-wall-sanctum where her voice echoed, indifferent to thousands of voices, where her voice blew out the others with a single puff, where she was deaf and blind but not mute, and her condition made her stammer into the void and chew her fingernails and know she was alone only by not hearing herself, not knowing whether the words came out of her mouth or ran like trains through her imagination.

Three knocks on the door made her snap shut like a clam.

"Who is it?"

Iván's voice, a hand grabbing her by the hair.

"Come on out of your bat cave, güey. They beat the shit out of El Cuco."

Interviewee: El Cuco Martínez

Location: Sor Rita Bar, Carrer de Mercè, 27, 08002, Barcelona

"I don't know if she translated them from French to Spanish or English to Spanish or German to Spanish. Fuck, I don't even know how many languages the tía spoke. She was doing it to make a little cash because the FONCA grant wasn't cutting it."

"Right."

"I thought it was funny she was always holed up in her room, supposedly writing a novel, which is, you could say, an intellectual thing to do . . . What do I know, would you say it's intellectual? I dunno. She seemed like one of these tormented types. She fit the bill. I mean the Kafka stereotype, not the Hemingway one. She was kinda sickly. She stayed up late. I did too, but at least I kept the light on. The glow of the screen was enough for her. She was a fucking bat. Whatever. I thought it was funny she was always holed up in there, supposedly writing a novel, and then, at the end of the day, she'd sit down to translate that stuff."

"There are different sides to people."

"I know, I know, but it's funny, if you think about it."

"Could you not smoke, please."

"Sorry, man. I didn't know it bothered you."

"My mother died of lung cancer. I saw her slowly turn into a sheet of cardboard. I can't get the image out of my head."

"Sorry."

"Don't worry about it. Go on."

"Well, I don't know what else to tell you."

"I want to know everything: What was it like living with them, what did they do, what did they say? Everything."

"I dunno, I dunno. I'd never lived with Latin Americans. It's not like I have anything against Latin Americans. I wouldn't be talking to you if I did, but you can already tell I'm not that kind of guy. It's just that I'd never lived with people from the other side, that's all, and it ended up broadening my horizons, let's put it that way. The truth is the apartment was pretty affordable between the six of us. The rooms were small and nice. They had student cards, but the siblings, the Ecuadorians, your compatriots, they never went to the university. They always skipped class. That's how I ended up getting a lot closer to them than to the Mexicans."

"Iván and Kiki are the Mexicans?"

"Yeah, that's right."

"And you weren't in school."

"No. What for?"

"But you did go to school before. I understand you have a degree in video game design."

"Oh, that. Yes, but I never graduated."

"Right."

"Back then I was in love with this nerdy girl who convinced me to go to school for something. The truth is I didn't really need it. Everything I learned in video game design I could have learned on my own, in my room, with a computer and internet access. It isn't hard if you try. Besides, I'm good with computers. Her name was Lola. She studied psychology, and her dad was a retired military man. When I went over to her house for dinner, I had to dress up like a nerd and put up with all sorts of right-wing bullshit. He was the typical tío with a white mustache who always does the top button of his shirt, so you feel like you're being strangled just by looking at it because how can this tío even breathe with his neck all squeezed red like that. His face got red too, not just his neck. And when he lifted his wineglass to drink, the pale skin of his hand, which looked like a plucked chicken, contrasted with his tomato-colored neck and face. I realize now that I've been calling that mass of fat supporting his head a neck just so you'll understand, but more than a neck, it looked like an extension of his face deformed by the weight of his flesh. It wasn't a pretty sight, tío, but obviously I couldn't say that to my girl. Most of the time I didn't even hear what he said, which was most certainly bullshit along the lines of None of this happened when Franco was around. I'd just stare at his enormous, overripe tomato face, and I'd be startled to see features and expressions hidden under the fat that I'd later see in Lola. I could never sleep with her after we'd gone to her parents' house. It was impossible. I don't think she ever noticed, or at least she didn't dwell on it if she did. I'm sure she never would've guessed that I didn't want to sleep with her because I was afraid I'd see her father while we were doing it. Maybe Lola figured the emotional effort I put into those dinners left me exhausted and that's why we never slept together afterward, but that wasn't the reason: I was afraid of seeing her father in the look on her face in the middle of . . . well, you get it. I never would've gotten over something like that. It would've been like fucking the man himself. It would have taken a millisecond to spot a resemblance between my girlfriend and her progenitor, a millisecond, you get it? And it could happen while she twisted up her features, anticipating the explosion of an orgasm like a rocket, tío, from her parted lips. I would've died. I'm not exaggerating. Something inside me would've died forever."

"I get it. And what happened with the girlfriend?"

"We broke up. Lola loved her father, and I looked down on her for it, because what kind of person could have positive feelings for a retired military man, someone nostalgic for Franco, someone who said things like, Black men smell bad because it's their race, their skin color that makes them stink like a wet goat, someone who generally hated immigrants, and who was proud to have played the cornet as a young man in who knows how many processions of the Christ of the Good Death. Every time she invited me over for dinner at their house, Lola forced me to dress like someone else, the boyfriend her father would've wanted me to be. I had to say I was Catholic and a law student. If that asshole had known I was actually studying video game design, he would've kicked me out of the house. He would've done the same thing if he had known I don't give a damn about God or all the saints in his fucking shitty church, or if I'd dressed like this, like I am now, the way I always dress. He was the worst kind of facha."

"Sorry, facha?"

"Facha. Fascist. Everything was rotten in that family. Lola's mom was always a shadow, for instance. And I don't mean that poetically or anything. I'm speaking very literally. The woman never spoke but somehow always arranged things to sit on the side of the table with the least amount of light so you could hardly see her. During dinner, she was like a dark, blurry stain that would move about as if she had a basket of fruit or something on her head, a weight that forced her to stand ramrod straight and make no sudden movements. Strangely, Lola and her father acted as if she weren't there, which made her even shadowier. When she got up to look for something or get something from the kitchen, she'd never turn on the light. She'd step into the darkness of the kitchen, submerging in it as if into her turtle shell, then emerge as if nothing had happened and sit back down on the least-lit side of the table. It was the same thing when she'd go to the living room or upstairs: she'd never turn on the light. It was like she could only see in the dark."

"What can I say: it doesn't sound like this Lola could have turned out great in an environment like that."

"I dunno, I dunno. This is going to sound strange, but she and I never talked about important stuff. Or at least I don't remember doing so. I couldn't tell you any opinion she had on anything. For all I know, Lola was just as much of a fascist as her father. I guess I was afraid to find out, so I never asked about anything that might make her tell me about the world as she saw it. She wasn't at all like her mother. Although sometimes I got the sense she had shadows of her own, which was why she insisted on staying in the light. I dunno, I dunno. This may sound like I'm losing it, but I think her father abused her. She never told me directly, but she always avoided giving details about her childhood and would only say that her father had made a lot of mistakes when she was little because he drank a lot, but it was all behind them now. Once I risked it and asked her: Did your father abuse you? And she smiled like one of those terrifying plastic dolls and said: My father is the best father in the whole wide world. But I saw her hands tremble and knew there was something rotten there, that there was a skeleton in the family's closet and Lola had gotten used to the stench. We broke up soon after because her father realized I was stealing stuff from his house. The truth is I wasn't too upset about the breakup. Mostly because in my mind I'd created a monstrous portrait of her family, and Lola had slowly started creeping into the picture. In any case, when the siblings gave me the video to upload to the online game, I thought about Lola again and felt guilty: Asshole, you could have done something! I said to myself. And I started to go crazy thinking that maybe she was waiting for me to rescue her from the love she felt for her father, an unconditional love that only made her sick, and that's why she always insisted I go to her house for dinner, so I'd rescue her, so I could see it with my own eyes, and all I did was spy on the skeleton in the closet and then leave and wash my hands of the matter."

"But you don't know if that really happened. You don't know if your ex-girlfriend experienced some kind of abuse when she was a child or if you're imagining it. I get the sense that you hated this person so much you wanted to believe he was a child abuser on top of everything else."

"Of course, it's totally possible. And that's what I told myself when I was feeling guilty. I told myself she'd never confessed anything of the sort to me, that I was just making assumptions. But then I'd drive myself crazy thinking that maybe if I hadn't been so blind or so focused on myself, maybe I would've seen signs, things that would've made me understand the shadow inside Lola. I thought if I'd cared more about her, if I'd listened more closely, if I'd studied her like I do a map when I'm lost, then maybe her pain, which she never put into words but I sometimes found lurking in things she said, would've been tangible for me. Then I could've done something to relieve it, like tearing her out of her father's arms, making her see that the love she felt for him was self-deception, that she actually hated him for what he'd done to her when she was little. I dunno, I dunno."

"But you still uploaded those videos to the Deep Web. You created the game and uploaded the videos, even though it made you think of Lola and everything you're telling me."

"Man, that was different. That was something else. The siblings decided they wanted the videos in the game and the game on the Deep Web, and I couldn't say no. Who would've said no to them? And if they walked through that door right this second and asked me again, I'd do it again, because you can't say no to the victims of that kind of thing."

Iván Herrera, age 25. Master in literary creation.

Room #2

You woke to the smell of ammonia from the almost-dry sweat on your skin. The first thing you did was look at yourself: a greasy, shiny layer coated your body and glued your skin to the bedsheets; a second skin, a smooth white gift. You unstuck your body from the fabric and stood up only to see the replica of the Shroud of Turin you'd left on the mattress. You wished the silhouette were less grotesque, that the smell of your sweat were fainter, that your penis weren't erect and pointing toward the door. It was nine in the morning. The sun was burning in every corner, but it wasn't the heat that made you sweat. You'd dreamt again that you were in Coatzacoalcos, at the port, naked by the river with no one around you, just the breeze drying your lungs and moistening your hands. The sun was a blinking eye that left you in darkness for brief flickers of time, like a little boy fiddling with a light switch. You tried to coordinate the blinking of the sun with the movement of your own eyelids so you wouldn't have to see the landscape switching on and off. You were waiting, though you didn't know for what or for whom, watching the horizon. Your erect penis wriggled like a serpent between your legs, but this wasn't strange to you: you were Quetzalcoatl, the plumed serpent, god and life of all men. You stood firm while a canoe carrying a dark specter glided toward the port. You could only make out his silhouette as he neared land and started walking toward you. You recognized yourself in him, the loathsome-you, and you looked into the imageless mirror he held in his hands, a mirror radiating clouds. You allowed your duality, your nemesis, Tezcatlipoca, to approach you. You allowed the black hands coming out of the mirror to grasp your serpent and shake it. You let out a moan when the mouth of the loathsome-you encircled your member with its tongue and saliva. The sky is a cyclops and the sun its eye, you thought when Tezcatlipoca ripped off your penis in a single bite and spat it into the river. As the blood spread crimson through the water and purified it, you smiled: now you were only feathers, now you could fly. And that's where the dream always ended.

You got into the shower and scrubbed your body as if you were beating it, which may have been what you were doing, deep down. You wanted the water to tear apart your muscles and break your bones, but you were still there, David, Quetzalcoatl, smoking black mirror, unharmed by the rigidity of nature. When you finally left the room, you found only closed doors. A tiny, deserted space, a common area with magazines, newspapers, a nail file, a DVD of *Pink Flamingos*, a pair of striped shoes, a black Joy Division shirt, the portrait of Laura Palmer, two novels by Diamela Eltit, one by Jorge Enrique Adoum, three packs of Oreos, a cigarette buried in ashes, a candy wrapper, a pink square candle, a trail of crumbs around the end table, three wine stains on the gray couch, four empty glasses with smudges from fingers and lips, a crumpled napkin. You turned your back on the chaos. Nothing in the world would make you clean up this disaster others had created. You left without breakfast and took the bus that would drop you off at the university. Your penis tried to stiffen twice on the way, first pointing toward a man with a tattoo covering his face and then toward a man with a beard and hairy arms, but you concentrated on the lines in the book by Onetti and on what you would do to your rebellious member when night came and your arousal wilted. Sometimes, especially on the bus, you'd feel phantom breasts bouncing against your ribs, and the sensation sent a flutter of pleasure across your chest. Your body was full of imaginary prostheses. You were missing organs, and no one knew.

You entered the classroom ten minutes after the lecture started and sat down, as always, in the back row. The professor was talking about Montaigne, the literary essay, Rafael Sánchez Ferlosio, Octavio Paz, the hybridization of genres, film, Manuel Puig, but you were looking at your classmates' backs and realizing you could only recognize them that way, from behind, because their faces were nebulous, enveloped in smoke. Their necks and shoulders, on the other hand, had first and last names. You remembered the first time you were attracted to someone: you were twelve years old, and he went to school with you. You'd never really seen him before. His eyes, his nose, his hair, were like everyone else's eyes, noses, and hair. But one day he sat down in the chair in front of yours and filled the space with his back, one you'd never bothered to look at until then. The teacher handed out the exams, and everyone but you bent their heads over the colorless pages, focused, mute, absent, but your eyes were anchored on the back centimeters from your nose, a back a little wider than your own, with long, delicate shoulders, a spine that made you want to reach out and touch it, to sink your fingers in, to bite, and your body shuddered and your mouth filled with thick saliva that tasted like rubber. You didn't know why you were shaking. You didn't know the shaking was desire. Since then, that love was a back and nothing more. Even today you wouldn't be able to remember the boy's face or the texture of his hair or the color of his eyes. Rohmer's film *Claire's Knee* reminded you of your localized desire, your longing for a part of your first love's body. You never again fell in love with anyone's back. The twenty-five people now showing you their necks didn't make so much as a hair stir. Thirty-something Omar Barciona, who always wore tight shirts to show off his muscles, was sitting five rows in front of you. You could see his vertebrae through the fabric. He was Argentine and found a way to mention his numerous readings of Joyce's *Ulysses* every time he raised his hand, even when it wasn't relevant. You imagined him tied to your bed, facedown, as you stuck wrinkled pages of *Ulysses* up his ass. The image made you smile, but the happiness was short-lived because your penis straightened up in your pants, a monster in rigor mortis. Not even the paralyzing waves of disgust could quell the erection. You weren't disgusted by what had aroused you—Omar's ass penetrated by pages of Joyce; the ink of a philosophical language absorbed by a painfully mediocre rectum—but by your member, that wet serpent that felt foreign to you, an invader of your body, which you hated more than anything else in the world. And there it was, pressing against the fabric, reminding you that it existed and you couldn't get rid of it. Tezcatlipoca. The loathsome-you. You tried to concentrate on your classmates' heads: feather dusters, fronds, sponges, ponytails. Fingernails with chipped blue polish scratched a neck and left red lines on the skin. Two shoulders rose and dropped. A head flung back. A back curved forward like a hook. The only face in the class was that of the professor, who was now talking about *Tristram Shandy;* an egg-shaped, evasive face that always showed its shadowed profile just like an actor performing a monologue on a poorly lit stage. No one in the class knew how much you hated your erect penis, how much you wanted to rip it off and throw it down the toilet. It was an enormous leech sucking the life out of your pelvis. Only your body, that larva, could generate the thirst for violence that now forced you to grab your pencil and bring it under the table. The professor with a head like a limp chili, sucker of Muslim and Jewish cocks, kept talking about Sterne's novel, but he, having done doctoral research on Sebald and destruction, he who had a master's in comparative literature and another in theoretical studies, he who had an undisguisable bald patch that reflected the bright white light suspended from the ceiling, and various articles published in specialized journals, and perfectly ironed pants with a crease down the middle, he who talked with a Montblanc pen in his fingers that he sometimes brought to his mouth like the great sodomitic son of a bitch he was, and who had written an article about female Latin American writers in the twentieth century, his shirt tucked into his pants like a fucking fascist and wrinkled by a brown belt with a gold buckle, he who was now talking about Montaigne again, with thick hairs on the back of his hand, a band on his left ring finger, he who wrote reviews for various cultural supplements, who drove a dark-blue metallic Mercedes-Benz, and had large, perfectly straight teeth, and wore shit-colored moccasins, a white shirt, and a gray tie, he who had done research on American women writers from the colonial period, he who had a Strellson Balham black leather briefcase, a Rolex that left marks on his wrist, a facsimile of the *Divine Comedy* on his desk, couldn't know anything about literature. A man like that, square, impeccable, comfortable with himself, comfortable with his life, his career, his income, his reputation as a tight-ass, couldn't understand that literature was vomit ejected by people like you, people full of duplicities and masks. You slowly pushed the tip of your pencil against the fabric of your pants until it reached the flesh of your member. None of the backs in front of you could ever make anything worthwhile, because they lived in a comforting fantasy that made them feel like survivors. Only you, driving the tip of your pencil into your erect penis and disguising the pain with a plaster-like expression without knowing why, since no one was looking at you, not even the professor with Ralph Lauren glasses, and you felt the heat of victory embracing your feathered heart while your serpent coiled up, docile, repentant, only you could know about survival and write things that would make sense in a world of cynical placidity. You and people like Kiki or the Terán siblings or even El Cuco, people who lived in discomfort, in exhaustion, not those who turned their backs to you, not that fag who drank Vichy water and then set the bottle down next to his Strellson Balham briefcase, you, the loathsome-you, even though your parents supported you in Europe, sending you money from beautiful Mexico, lovely Mexico, even if you were from Polanco and your bother said *cool* and *nice* in English more times in a single sentence than you could count. You could be the one with Ralph Lauren glasses and the Rolex if that's what you wanted, but you'd been chosen to be Quetzalcoatl and to have your smoking black mirror, your nemesis, incarnated like a thorn under your wing. Your penis had withdrawn into its folds, but you continued to poke it in case it decided to get up again. You were dirty inside. You were a torturer and a victim. You watched Carla Rodríguez stick a piece of chewing gum under the table and press it with her index finger in 180-degree rotations, only to wipe her finger on her long red summer skirt made from fabric that looked like corrugated paper, rigid to the eye's touch. Because the gaze does touch, you thought, but no one caressed you with their eyes. You felt ferocious and heroic for resisting the pain of the pencil tip on your coiled ophidian member. Tomás Fuentes opened a note-book with lined pages and drew spirals from the inside out, whirl-winds that started to make you dizzy, metaphoric notes on the uninterrupted orality of the professor who'd written an essay about literature and censorship during the Franco dictatorship and who preferred *The Anatomy of a Moment* by Cercas to his *Soldiers of Salamis*. The classroom was a poorly lit rectangle where the light had to be kept on during the day. Five, nine, thirteen, fifteen, seventeen people had a novel or a book of poems on the table that defined them or that they wanted to define them, like an ID card, and they only put the book on the table so others would see it, because they didn't have to bring anything to class, not even a notebook. It was enough to listen to the voice that the Vichy water didn't clear, the filthy voice that, over the course of the year, had given a talk on Eros and exoticism in Thomas Mann's work, two lectures on Coetzee and the responsibility of the intellectual and his fucking mother, a course on the narrative work of Cristina Peri Rossi, and which had also organized a round-table with Mathias Énard. Your legs tensed. The tip of the pencil was a lance against your flaccid flesh. The shirts of some of your class-mates had adhered to their backs and darkened with the heat ema-nating from their bodies. Thick, indecent drops ran between your thighs, moistening the place where your phantom vulva began. Elisa Ulloa had three tiny curls clinging to her long virgin neck, the twisted neck of the modernist swan, bent toward Javier "the trembling" Bas, whose sick-of-betraying-him hands shivered in the thirty-five-degrees-Celsius heat. You wanted to be brave enough to drive the pencil into yourself, to *dismember yourself,* so everyone would call you sick and crazy as if they knew what sickness and craziness were, as if they suddenly knew something about the loathsome-you, about the smoking black mirror, and they'd judge you and your imaginary prostheses, your hatred of your living flesh hanging from the not-your-body, with that disharmonious but solid certainty of those who learn through repetition, through rhythm, and don't ever dare to break their stride. The backs before you couldn't touch you with their eyes, and they didn't want to. No one in that class would understand the pencil against your weapon of Mexican masculinity, established by the Revolution as an object of national pride. No one would understand that you were shaping yourself, educating your body, or that discipline became possible through punishment; that you, like the Greeks, believed in the dietetics of the pleasures and in the domestication of the not-your-body. Beatriz Tello López used her outstretched pinky to remove a long, curly blond hair resting on her green satin blouse. For your master's thesis, you'd write something simple, something like *Le carnet de Rose* by Alina Reyes: fragments in which you'd talk about the loathsome-you and the transfiguration of your penis. You believed the French writer was right when she wrote these lines you liked so much in *The Butcher*: "Flesh is not sad, it is sinister. It belongs on the left side of our souls, it catches us at times of the greatest abandonment, carries us over deep seas, scuttles us and saves us; flesh is our guide, our dense black light, the well which draws our life down in a spiral, sucking it into oblivion." Flesh: your sinister side, the loathsome-you, Tezcatlipoca. You thought about Kiki, the true writer, to whom you'd once confided that you were training yourself to resist the pain of your transfiguration. She'd said, tweezing invisible hairs from her face, that she thought what you were doing was brave, and even though she was really just telling you things from the bitchiest place of ignorance, you believed her, because she'd managed to tell you something that was true to you, a truth in your inner world that she'd somehow transmuted on her Malinchean tongue to be articulated and pronounced in a simple but performative way. You eased pressure on the pencil, and as you pulled it away from your Quetzalcoatl serpent, a thin, invisible pain like a razor's edge crept up and down your now docile, now sleeping member, making you tear up and drool like a dog. You'd been chosen to live with a true writer to make you realize you'd never be one, even though you understood more about literature than all the backs in your class, even though you were broken, unbalanced, peripheral, and therefore capable of offering a story that subverted the order of the chairs and position of the tables in classroom 20.003. The difference between Kiki and you was that she wanted to write (herself) to understand (herself) while you needed to disarm(or) yourself to better know yourself. You knew writing couldn't tell you anything about your flesh. Only pain was capable of constructing a discourse of the not-your-body, but pain was nontransferable and inexpressible for the purposes of language. Hugo Llach scratched his armpit right where a greenish-yellow mark had settled onto his skin. Who would turn around to look at you, touch you, prick you, berate you, plunge their cock into your Casper-like vulva? Who would disrupt the order of the chairs? You hoped the professor would set down his Montblanc pen one day and sully his hands with a piece of chalk to write something important, something Kiki would tell you, something about the essence of literature, about shaking up old structures, about how important it was to break molds, to do things with words, but they didn't talk about that in your class, they didn't talk in any of your classes about why writing meant living in a place of tension and discomfort, they didn't touch on the only important thing about literary creation, and that's why the backs in front of you believed that writing was just a pretty phrase. The creation of your *I* began with violence, and there wasn't anything beautiful about the process, or maybe there was, but how would they ever understand it? How would they ever understand you if they couldn't even pronounce you?

Interviewee: Kiki Ortega

Location: El Gato del Raval, Rambla del Raval, 08001, Barcelona

"If you ask me, I'd say all Westerners take part in BDSM culture."

"Really?"

"And by Western I also mean us, the Mexican kids on the ground floor of the American continent. Even though they don't see us as Westerners, we belong to that same BDSM culture."

"Mexico is in North America."

"No. Well, it depends what geography you're talking about. We Mexicans are the South even though we're in the North, y'know? We're like you Ecuadorians. We're the continent's basement. Well, let's say we're the basement steps and you all are the basement itself."

"Yes, that's a good way of looking at it."

"But we have to ask ourselves what unites us. And what unites us, beyond language and our colonial past and all that bullshit, is that we're raised Christian. It doesn't matter if we believe in Jesus, the dove, the little God who removes sins from the world, the always-virginal-Mary, and the rest of that fuckery. What matters is that we all grew up with the same images: Jesus nailed to a cross, his gaze wrenched toward the sky, his crown of thorns, and the blood running down his face like a spring. We were all told that this is beautiful and mysterious, that this—to die, to sacrifice yourself, to submit your body to the most horrible torments because of and for someone else—is love. They've been fucking us over with that since the beginning, but when you're screwed from such a young age, you don't even realize it, you grow up thinking that's just how things are, it's normal. I still remember when my grandmother took me to church for the first time. They had the goriest sculpture of Jesus on the cross.

I was a girl in a place where I wasn't allowed to talk, surrounded by suffering faces that freaked me out. It didn't matter where I looked, there were faces with twisted eyes all over the place, the same grimaces we were forced to identify as sacred. My grandmother told me I had to love those grimaces because they loved me. What she was really saying, unbeknownst to her, was that I should love the pain those images represented and feel it in my own flesh so I could purify myself. Güey, just walk into a church and you'll see what I mean. Everyone goes there to suffer, at least for a few minutes, because it gives them spiritual pleasure. They're like this because they've grown up with the narrative that to achieve love, you have to purify yourself through pain, because beauty is associated with the blood and expressions of Christian martyrs. Love and pain are interchangeable concepts as far as they're concerned. Have you ever been to Seville?"

"No, I haven't."

"Well, you should go. They have lots of virgins. My favorite is Nuestra Señora de la Esperanza Macarena, or La Macarena. She's worth seeing in person: there are glassy teardrops trickling down her cheeks, and her eyebrows look like two wings about to open in flight. Never in my life have I seen a sculpture with such a vivid look on its face. Her eyes walk the line between sadness and terror. Maybe that's why I like it. It's really cool. During Holy Week, she's surrounded by an impossible congregation of people immersed in a collective catharsis. The processions are held to demonstrate the pain and sacrifice that, for the devout, is the same as the purest expression of love. The costaleros bear all the weight of the statues mounted on the floats, and they do it voluntarily, thrilled to march while shouldering who knows how many tons. What in other circumstances would be torture, a clear violation of human rights, becomes a cleansing ritual during Holy Week. I mean, it's the twenty-first century, güey! The float could be put on a cart and easily driven on four wheels, but the costaleros still exist and offer their shoulders, risking injuries or even broken bones, and no one finds it strange or masochistic. When I saw it for the first time in Mexico, I thought: You've got to be kidding me. It's so fucked up."

"I see."

"Nuestra Señora de la Encarnación, who represents the Virgin Mary in the moment the word of God is incarnated in her womb, is also interesting. It's quite a literary question, language becoming flesh. In any case, this virgin is also called La Esclava del Señor because of Mary's response to the angel Gabriel: 'You see before you the Lord's servant; let it happen to me as you have said.' Slavery, submission to an all-powerful lord and master—doesn't that sound like BDSM to you?"

"When you put it that way . . ."

"What I'm getting at is that a lot of things we find perverse can become sublime, for some people in the art of Christian iconography, and for others in literary, visual, or performance art. Saints like Margaret Mary Alacoque, who claimed to experience bouts of mystical ecstasy, ate sick people's vomit and shit or even their own. Mary Alacoque felt God speak to and enter her through these acts. She was convinced that through the torment of the flesh she would attain saintliness, a near-divine state, and this gave her pleasure, let's be real. And now you must be wondering, how can a tortured body feel pleasure? Well, the answer is both simple and complex. It's not like I've gone through this kind of illuminating experience myself, but I have an imagination, and I've thought a lot about these things. I'm also very empathetic, even with people who have nothing to do with me. But let's get back to the point: the pleasure of a wounded and/ or humiliated body. It isn't really the physical suffering that makes these saints attain ecstasy. Suffering is just one way they can reach it. Pleasure isn't in the wounds of the flesh but in the idea of wounds of the flesh, and what it means. So what does it mean, you ask. Well, it means absolute surrender, total submission. For the saints who inflicted all sorts of physical punishment on themselves, there was nothing more arousing than sacrificing their bodies for their love: lord and master. I know I've only given examples of women, but you could say the same of all religious men who lash themselves, or the Filipinos who crucify themselves every year during Holy Week. Lidwina of Schiedam spent practically her entire life lying in bed, self-inflicting wounds as serious as ulcers, gangrene, stigmata, and dislocated joints, and she did it because through illness, through the mortification of her own body, she attained ecstasy, which was nothing but an orgasm produced by the significance of her carnal pain. BDSM was a part of Christianity long before Sacher-Masoch wrote *Venus in Furs,* but it's only considered perverse when it isn't associated with Christianity. What's the difference between a mystic saint and a woman who asks her partner to pour hot wax on her back and stick his fist up her ass? Maybe the difference is that the mystic saint, like the crucified man in Holy Week, is capable of self-destruction to reach ecstasy, while many BDSM enthusiasts are only playing at surrender."

"Well . . ."

"Samois, the pro-BDSM lesbian organization founded by Pat Califia, was heavily criticized by the WAVPM puritans because, they claimed, BDSM promoted violence toward women, when in reality violence, pain, pleasure, love, submission, sacrifice, are all notions we're taught from a young age through Jesus Christ Our Lord and Saint Mary, Mother of God. The idea that we understand love and pleasure any other way is a lie. That's how we were educated."

"Don't tell me you thought what the siblings did was normal because of this whole history of BDSM and Western culture."

"I don't think there's anything wrong with creating an online game, if that's what you're talking about. But if what you actually want to talk about is the business they ran, I don't know anything about it. Seriously, I haven't even been on the website. But if you want to know my opinion, I'm in favor of piracy."

"You and Iván were some of the first to play *Nefando.*"

"The Pirate Bay is proof that big film producers and distributors will never win against piracy as civil disobedience. When the police issued the warrant to the Pirate Bay and arrested its three administrators, the pro-piracy movement got even stronger. They couldn't charge people who created a BitTorrent tracker that worked through a P2P system for piracy because, technically, they weren't the ones reproducing copyrighted materials—the users of the tracker were. We were all pirates, like something in *Fuenteovejuna.* In our

Latin America, it's a different story. We Mexicans have Tepito, the Peruvians Polvos Azules, in Ecuador you have La Bahía, and so on. We have to find some way to make film accessible and employ people at the same time."

"You think the siblings were democratizing culture and opening the tap for everyone, that they were three Robin Hoods, when really they were lining their pockets."

"They wanted to make money, yes. And what's wrong with that? Let's not moralize such a complex question. The administrators of the Pirate Bay also make money off what they do, but that's nothing compared to the fortunes other companies make by exploiting people."

"Look, what I'm really interested in is *Nefando*. Would you tell me about that?"

"Why don't you search the gamer forums for the accounts of people who've played it? It's become a landmark, at least for some. Anything I could tell you will be there."

"Little to nothing is said about *Nefando* on the indexed internet."

"No shit! Everyone who played *Nefando* navigates at the very bottom of the ocean, man. If you want to find a dragonfish, you should scuba dive where the light doesn't shine."

"Wouldn't it be easier to just tell me?"

"No, güey. But for real, are you scared?"

El Cuco Martínez, age 29. Hacker. Scener. Video game designer.

La Rambla wasn't a promenade, it was the sea, and all the people were waves that were going to spill into the port, but only once he'd chosen them as his prisoners or loosed them into the sweaty human current of flyers and Catalan flags, postcards from the Sagrada Familia, La Pedrera, Casa Batlló, and Park Güell, posters of Camp Nou, miniature sculptures of castells, Dios Messi jerseys, floating human statues, portrait painters with black hands, carcass-esque-caricaturists, musicians, and thieves. El Cuco leaned against a lamppost outside La Boqueria market and watched the swells of tourists wearing explorer hats and smears of sunscreen on their baby-bottom-cheeks. A few meters away, close to a kiosk, stood La Rata; his eyes carefully followed the flow of people until he suddenly clung like a limpet to the haunches of a couple sporting Quechua backpacks. Once La Rata was able to unzip a pocket and extract something valuable, he'd hand it off to Montero, always on a diagonal from their prey, and Montero would pass the baton to him. Only then would El Cuco abandon his post and leap into La Boqueria or down a side street adjoining La Rambla to meet up with Javi or Rubén, dressed as students with full backpacks, and that would be the end of the source code.

The function was simple:

```
#include <stdio.h>
int main () {
// camouflage chameleon
int La Rata, Montero, El Cuco, Javi or Rubén, Xenophobic
Anti-Tourist Union, Quechua backpacks, result;
```

```
La Rata= 1;
Montero= 2;
El Cuco= 3;
Javi or Rubén= 4;
Quechua backpacks= 10;
// sum chameleon efforts
Xenophobic Anti-Tourist Union= La Rata+Montero+El
Cuco+Javi
or Rubén;
result= Quechua backpacks-Xenophobic Anti-Tourist Union;
printf ("%d - %d= %d", Quechua backpacks, Xenophobic
Anti-Tourist Union, result);
return 0;
}
```

But he shoved his hands into his pockets when he saw La Rata move away from the lobster-colored couple and discreetly pause at the closest kiosk. Two policemen were walking by a few meters away, laughing, going against the stream of the crowd, their shoulders thrust forward, their backs spoon-like, a veil of iridescent sweat on their rag faces, and their thumbs hooked on their gun belts. They didn't even look at La Rata. Being Spanish was useful when it came to scaring people who think you have to be foreign to steal. The surprise factor—rabbit skin, average European height, lagoon eyes—played in the group's favor; the sun, exhaustion, and Arab presence on the perimeter did too. For life to be harmonious, he thought, frowning, it should be a string of algorithmically organized events. El Cuco believed in the language of instructions, in its imperative syntax, the logic of prepositions, and its power to execute desires. His personal motto, found in a 4 kB intro, was that variables never pose a real challenge if you have complete command of the constants. Programming, being a scener, had taught him to manipulate the constants at his whim and apply creativity to precarious instruments. That's how he was able to easily make five hundred euros in a day and a top-notch intro in a tiny 64 kB size. The demoscene world was born to thieves like him,

people labeled as cyber pirates but who were really more revolution-
aries than criminals. The hacker ethic answered to a few basic values:
creativity and freedom. This made him feel he was walking the walk
when he met with the Xenophobic Anti-Tourist Union in La Rambla
or on the Barceloneta beach because he could proudly say that his
time spent in the fresh air or at his computer obeyed the same moral
code and that his life lacked any fundamental contradictions—
nothing mattered more to him than the formal logic of functions.
The first crackers from the eighties, the forefathers of the demoscene,
made a name for themselves with little intros that consisted of some
sketch hovering around a pseudonym placed at the beginning of the
cracked video game. Those intros became increasingly elaborate and
of a higher quality than the games they were supposedly introduc-
ing. That's when the sceners emerged, a smaller group that decided to
create true works of art through algorithms. El Cuco was only twelve
when he discovered the demoscene world. His uncle was a self-taught
computer scientist who attended demoparties, and he occasionally
brought El Cuco along to show him what his hobby was all about. El
Cuco remembered watching, with timid interest, the intros projected
by five scener groups. At the time he didn't understand the complex-
ity of the work that went into making the images and music stored
in a lightweight executable file. It felt like watching music videos by
Gorillaz or Daft Punk or, when the pixels were visible, demos from
PC games like *Dangerous Dave*. There was something mystical about
those pieces that shook him to his core; the mystery, the veiled logic
was the operating system that let him see and listen to the projected
intros: the language of the instructions, the written code. His uncle
introduced him to the world of programming, and he soon managed
to make his first rotating cube with textures and colors like those
from *Dangerous Dave*. Before El Cuco could finish his 64 kB intro
with two hypercubes, a hypersphere, three polytopes, a hexakis octa-
hedron, and an octagonal trapezohedron, his uncle died from a heart
attack. He was found at his Commodore Amiga keyboard, where he
was using a tracker to compose the soundtrack for his nephew's debut
piece. From then on, and with the intention of always maintaining

his creative independence, El Cuco was clear about his decision never to join a scener group. With fervent obstinacy he decided to be a coder, musician, graphic artist, modeler, and designer. To be everything was to be God. He frequently told the Xenophobic Anti-Tourist Union that as a subculture, the demoscene was forged by the fingers of the first crackers and lived on in those who believed in the creative possibilities of an 8- or 16-bit computer. Crackers and sceners always felt the need to challenge limits by experimenting with the poetics of C language, virtual craftsmanship, coding style. It was all meant to share the results with the most people possible and to create the ideal conditions for a participative democracy grounded in action, not just language, one in which knowledge wouldn't be restricted to one group and in which others would be able to take the initiative. For El Cuco, programming was the perfect weapon of civil disobedience. It allowed you to do important things from where you sat, real things, not like in literature, the Terán siblings would say. Poetry can pose problems but not solutions, Irene claimed while lying in his bed. Writing in C language, on the other hand, demanded results, he thought. It was the language of action.

Montero put his headphones on and pretended to listen to music, maybe heavy metal because of the way he shook his head. He positioned himself next to a plump couple with swollen necks, mattress backs, arms like Joselito Gran Reserva hams, who had two Canon EOS 5D Mark III cameras hanging against their chests and squeaky-clean orthopedic sandals. Robbing French people or Germans who had enough money to bankroll a good vacation in Barcelona was nothing more than intervening in the fair redistribution of wealth, El Cuco often thought, so as to add a sense of social responsibility to his rhetoric. The Xenophobic Anti-Tourist Union didn't really have anything against foreigners and nothing against tourism. Aside from La Rata and Rubén, who nursed an ardent Catalanism and belonged to an extreme sect that organized oratory sessions in a gym and had participated in boycotts against immigrant businesses, none of the members flaunted their roots, which were really quite scattered, especially in El Cuco's case—his father was Basque, his mother Galician, and he, even though he was born in Seville, had lived in Madrid until he was eighteen before moving to Barcelona. Montero had come up with the group's name after they'd all decided to pickpocket distracted tourists who strolled down La Rambla and lay in the sun like pallid walruses on the Barceloneta beach, with the naïveté and nonchalance of the truly oblivious. Sometimes El Cuco would feel stabs of remorse when he unzipped a Quechua backpack, usually when it belonged to a tourist over fifty, with wrinkles etched like scars, a belly blocking the view of their feet, and teeth like chunks of yellow wax, or a backpack that belonged to someone traveling alone, clutching a map in their right hand, a handkerchief in their left, huge beads of sweat cascading down their forehead. You had to live somehow, though, and money doesn't grow on trees but in Quechua backpacks and the swollen pockets of Coronel Tapiocca pants. A nearby lesbian couple was arguing in Catalan about pornoterrorism and the ridiculous block on websites like GirlsWhoLikePorno in public libraries. They were weighing the possibility of organizing a flash mob and masturbating among the political philosophy shelves, because that way, said the girl with the horseshoe-shaped septum ring, they'd clearly express their objection to institutional censorship and to the misguided idea that pornography isn't a form of knowledge or an instrument for the subversion of the heteronormative imaginary suppressing them. The other girl, a Rastafarian in a Sex Pistols T-shirt, said that masturbating in the library could also open the eyes of everyone studying there, because silence generates nothing but ideas removed from reality and noise, ideas deaf to the shouts from unindexed, marginalized voices. El Cuco smiled and thought about his father; he'd only met him once—back when he hadn't yet learned to memorize the maps in people's faces—and knew nothing about him, except that he'd been in ETA and was sentenced to twenty years in a Dominican prison for drug trafficking. He suspected his father had never set foot in a public library, but he must know a lot more about subversion than those girls dreaming about masturbating against the spine of a book by Catharine MacKinnon. Some time ago, El Cuco had read the name Leche de Virgen Trimegisto in an online feminist magazine. Under the subtitle "Open Your Ass and You Will Open Your Mind," the article described, with overwhelming stylistic dexterity, his art form as centered on the abject, the scatological, the philosophy of horror, performance, the body as sculptural terrain, queer theory, contrasexuality, postpornography, pataphysics, esperpento, ultra-violence, theater of the cruel, ephemeral panic, transgression, the oneiric, counterculture, symbolic space, dystopia, new aesthetic languages, concluding with the syntagma-enigma "among others," which could only imply the absence of a true end to the magnum-description of a deific art. "All I know is he's a dude who pisses and shits and sticks things up his ass, just like everyone else, but because he does it onstage, he supposedly incites us to think about our body as a model we can use to arm ourselves against a political-cultural system that's always screwing us over," Kiki told him when he asked about Leche de Virgen Trimegisto. What was the body of his *I* submerged in a computer system? he wondered. Where did his subjectivity end and where did the subjectivity of everyone else begin in a virtual space? As El Cuco saw it, everyone was a performance artist on the internet, and for a brief spell, they were only mind and representation: pure politics. The on-screen representation was the most effective proof that the body could become a flat surface in order to project mental imagery, and that what was believed to be nature, immanence, was just an algorithmic construction ready to be innovated. Nothing did more to depoliticize the body than *to be* outside of *it,* to exist outside of its structure, El Cuco thought. Subverting the order through public masturbation, sticking things up your ass in front of a dozen people seemed more like exhibitionist acts than ones seeking real results, but he doubted those Annie Sprinkle devotees would agree. Making a spectacle of yourself was the opposite of censoring yourself, and they belonged to a generation that upheld a peculiar libertarian fantasy that spewed their hatred of institutional gags while furtively hoping to apply their own: gags they believed to be just, necessary, and progressive. El Cuco sometimes suspected it was only possible to live in a *Brave New World,* a cyclical dystopia in which, at the end of the day, organizational efficiency was all that mattered. So he was glad not to defend anything with such zeal that he'd want to statically mold the world like a stone house. He was glad to be himself and to live divided between dozens of discourses struggling to pile on top of one another, glad that this fighting urge was all he was really prepared to gamble.

As the plump couple laughed and photographed a caricature of Angela Merkel dressed as a dominatrix, Montero walked toward El Cuco, skipping La Rata, creating his own style of code, and handed him a wallet, or, as the Terán siblings might call it, a billfold—to rename is to re-create, as Kiki would say—which he stowed in his pocket while crossing the street to enter La Boqueria. El Cuco needed one hundred euros to pay for the Commodore Amiga 500 that a friend who had retired from the demoscene had offered him two weeks before. With some luck, he'd get the money that very afternoon, and then he could compose the music for his intros just like his uncle had; his uncle, who had been like a father to him, who had a heart so big it exploded in his chest, who was watching over him somewhere. That ghostly gaze was why El Cuco had been ashamed to masturbate as a teenager. For years his uncle's slight lazy eye had made him feel like he was being watched from every angle, every second of the day and night. Even though he locked himself in the bathroom or hid under the sheets, even though he knew it was impossible because a dead man is a dead man, even though he couldn't tell anyone, even though the sensation was like the terror people feel in the shadows, a terror caused by nothing in the outside world but by fear itself, illogical, irrational, yet somehow tangible to those who experience it; even though he knew the full truth, the root of his problem, the shame remained; the knowledge extinguished neither the fear nor the lazy-eyed gaze, because knowledge is sometimes just like a mirage, because imagination is a potentially macabre and destabilizing mechanism, because the sensation of being watched doesn't need a reason to exist, but it did exist, and that was enough.

El Cuco made his way through the market crowd with his uncle's acquiescent gaze over his shoulder and looked for Javi in the usual spot, next to the sole and blue lobsters. He found him chatting with the fisherman and holding a Curtis Garland novel. As he walked, a tall guy passed, maybe Arab, maybe Latin American, maybe Canarian, and turned around to look at him, not out of curiosity but to make sure he knew he was being watched by eyes other than his uncle's. When he finally shook Javi's hand and they said good-bye to the fisherman and left La Boqueria, heading toward the Plaça Sant Agustí, Javi told him that the maybe Arab, maybe Latin American, maybe Canarian man was actually one of the North Africans who worked in the same area as them and didn't like sharing their space or the tourists. El Cuco didn't say anything. He opened Javi's backpack, tucked the money in an inside pocket, and threw the wallet that belonged to the couple wearing Barça hats to shield themselves from the sun into a trash bin. Then he walked back to La Rambla and dove into the chaos and foul smells. Sometimes he believed his destiny was to be Henry Dorsett Case, a broken character who could only make sense of his life in his role as a cyber hacker, or John Difool, yet another mediocre guy in a deranged society run by the Techno-Technos. When his uncle died, El Cuco inherited a library full of science fiction novels and a box of comics by Moebius and Alan Moore. "To program, you need to have a world outside of programming," he jotted down in a text he read at a sceners meeting, "an alternate universe to sink your mind's teeth into, an image projected into the future that lets you think about the obsolescence of certain pillars that support us." On various occasions, especially when his mother developed an obsessive-compulsive disorder that forced her to group things in threes, he wished the empathy box described by Philip K. Dick in *Do Androids Dream of Electric Sheep?* were real, that there were a way to tap into the pain and happiness of others, so you suddenly became another person, embodied them, really loved them. He later understood that empathy has mental and technological limits, that people aren't made to laugh and cry for every person on earth, only a few, and that the closest thing he would ever have to the empathy box would be his computer with internet access, his computer that allowed him to extend his empathy a little beyond the limitations imposed by his corporality and his territoriality. How could he feel what the man holding a ferociously read Bible in his lap was feeling, the man with four wrinkles that ran across his forehead and down past his eyebrows, who looked like he was freezing to death in the sun, whose eyes got lost among so many tourists? How could he feel La Rata's hatred of immigrants and his even greater hatred of the Spaniards who wanted to rip the Catalan from his tongue and soul, a visceral hatred that took a back seat when El Cuco was involved, the only person he was willing to speak Spanish with? El Cuco liked to understand the frustration felt by the French and Germans they robbed when they realized, always too late, that someone had taken their money; putting himself in their shoes, he knew they'd be fine, that the bitter aftertaste would vanish after the shock, the rage, and the self-incrimination, that they'd go back to being happy in a foreign country, and that they'd probably get robbed again, because money is a necessary evil, just like the means of obtaining it.

That night, he promised himself, he'd finish the demo inspired by Isaac Asimov's made-up planet Solaria, land of isolation and extreme individualism, which he'd spent more than three months working on. El Cuco couldn't see why the great science fiction novels associated the idea of an individualistic dystopia with the existence of hyperdeveloped technology. For him, technology was a tool that granted people their humanity, that helped them come together rather than split apart. This union was achieved by representational means that sometimes allowed absurd hierarchies and ancient modes of communication to come unmasked. While its projections didn't always seem to get it right, science fiction was the only literary genre that interested him, because it was visionary, and because it demonstrated a clear understanding of how dangerous the human moral configuration really was. Science fiction literature, he felt, wasn't concerned with the fantasy of a nightmarish future, but with the reality of the present, where it finds elemental contradictions in behavioral norms and a lack of space for ethical reflection.

A few meters to his right, a circle of people with Colgate smiles had formed to watch two tourists getting conned by three con-artist-Fates. La Rata, Montero, and surely others pretended to watch the show while reaching into the spectators' open pockets. A man with an H. G. Wells mustache and a skinhead mien walked right past El Cuco. He smelled like rum and mold, but he was accompanied by a girl wearing a dress that barely covered her butt cheeks. El Cuco couldn't help but glance at the round bulges peeking out from the pink fabric and think about the hermaphroditism of Solaria's inhabitants and about how a recurring nightmare in science fiction is the strict control over sexual impulses and the elimination of any physical contact with others. The final eradication of our animal side—that which compels men and women to face the violence and savagery of their desires—was simultaneously utopian and dystopian. The concept of humanity is based on the systematic separation of mankind from its devastating nature and therefore from its Eros, he thought, trying to look at the sun. But humanity, he reflected, is much more than that: it's the attempt to reconcile the internal conflict between man and beast, intellect and instinct, life and death. This was his last thought before the North African guy from La Boqueria, along with two other Africans with long beards, walked past him with Javi's backpack. Javi appeared soon thereafter, sunken-eyed, saying they'd threatened him with a knife, saying they wanted them off their turf, next time they'd leave them dead, or almost dead, and they'd better not come back. James H. Jeans had said, El Cuco remembered at that moment, that the universe seemed less and less like a great thought and more and more like a great machine. And when La Rata and Montero joined them and heard Javi's story, they called Rubén, and La Rata, slightly flushed, said it was time to teach that Muslim brotherhood a lesson about the biggest tightwads in town, the ones who called the shots in Catalan territory. If the universe ran like a great machine, El Cuco thought, it also seemed like a crazed HAL 9000 or a Wintermute that threatened to become independent. But nobody cared, not even him.

Interviewee: Iván Herrera

Location: Starbucks, Col. Hipódromo Condesa, 06100, Mexico City

"What's the difference between a Mexican 'albur' and a Spanish 'albur'?"

"No idea."

"In Mexico, 'albur' is wordplay that can be a double or even triple entendre. It's all about ambiguity and depth. But for Spaniards 'albur' is risk, chance."

"I see."

"And what's the difference between the Ecuadorian 'cuco' and the Spanish 'cuco'?"

"I think I know this one."

"I'll tell you anyway: In Spain, 'cuco' is something beautiful, something sweet. But in your country, as you know, El Cuco is the monster that eats little kids who won't go to bed."

"Yes. And people sing to their kids: 'Sleep, little child, go to sleep now, El Cuco is coming and will eat you somehow.' The Teráns must have told you that?"

"Wait, do you believe in El Cuco?"

"What?"

"Güey, can't you tell, it's an albur."

The Hype Pornovela Library

CHAPTER ONE
By Kiki Ortega

I

For Diego, sex meant the lactic liquid erupting from his body like a vomit relinquishing him, if only for a few seconds, from his steadfast desire to die; it meant hurling his eyes inside his skull, a grove where panther shadows ran, and being perfect individuality: being flesh, skin, bones, blood. Being a body: being alive and not dead. But only when Eduardo's asshole opened, when he looked into the blind eye that could suck up the world if it wanted to, did he feel the urge to be contaminated individuality, bathed in the sludge of other bodies into which he could submerge his vermiform cock, his elegant cock, and only when his mouth opened to take Eduardo's pink dick and suck it and savor its fluids that tasted like an ocean of lava did he internalize an inexpressible knowledge that made him aware of his mysterious instincts once more.

And the mystery was as transparent as a foggy window.

II

Eduardo and Diego were eleven when they first opened their asses to one another. It happened during the wake for Diego's father. The two were standing together, looking at the feet of the only woman to have attended the funeral in open-toed high heels. Her red toenails contrasted with the black world that Diego's father's final death rattle had forged, a world of costumes all the color of eyelids, the color of question marks, and they were trying to make her uncomfortable by staring at her feet. Diego's mother scolded them, even though they weren't the only ones in the room staring at the woman's smiling toes, and sent them out to the garden, where everything was green except the ground with its thick grass veil. Diego told Eduardo that he'd seen his father's body's erect penis when they were dressing him. Eduardo told Diego that he'd seen his mother's vagina when she sat down without crossing her legs, and that, ever since, he always tried to catch a glimpse of this entrance, because it gave him butterflies and coated his underwear with a sticky liquid that he rubbed over his hands like soap when he touched his mother's clothes, clothes made of sweet smells, clothes he caressed and sighed into. Diego closed his eyes and imagined what it would be like to kiss Eduardo's mother's hidden lips, to kiss them the same way couples join their mouths and unite their tongues, only down there, Eduardo was saying, women don't have tongues. Then, like so many other times, they kissed by a tree with dry branches that pointed sunward like the giant tusks of a wild boar. They touched each other clumsily but with the greed for knowing. Revived, they went into the garden shed.

They confronted the pain of penetration with true hedonism; for them, sex was like everything else in childhood—an endurance test. Afterward, when the blood and shit stained them inside and out, they held their erect members and played swords.

III

When they were in seventh grade, they brought a girl to their shared room for the first time. She was twelve, they were thirteen. No one noticed at the boarding school. They took turns fucking her. First Eduardo, who was more delicate, and then Diego, who liked to stick it in hurriedly, forcefully, seized with a frenzy that made him pinch and hit the bodies he took. The girl ended up bruised, covered in semen, bite marks, and pools of saliva—Eduardo liked to spit on his lovers' skin. She cried at the sight of herself in the mirror. She broke down, her whole body shaking. Eduardo reminded her that she was the one who had wanted them to do what they did; that for months they'd been stealing glances at each other from opposing corners, kissing and touching where the teachers and supervisors couldn't see; that they'd shown her their robust cocks and she'd shown them her pink virgin vulva. The girl told him she knew and then fell into the deepest and most harmonious silence they'd ever heard. Diego lent her a novel by the Marquis de Sade that he'd taken from his dead father's library. Then she helped him draw nipples on Eduardo's naked body with his finger stained in the blood from her broken hymen.

The girl left school a week later.

IV

During the second semester, Diego and Eduardo noticed the PE teacher had taken a special interest in them. Whenever they did squats, ran laps around the soccer field, or played basketball, he'd watch them in a peculiar way, as if he wanted to pierce them with a language of silent and taciturn expressions. One night they followed him into the woods on the western side of the school. He was with a scrawny sixth grader who was shaking like a washing machine. The boy was wearing clean pajamas that looked like the moon: grayer than white, shinier than opaque. They went deep enough into the woods for the darkness to get into their lungs like a torrent of dirty water. Then the teacher stopped, grasped the sixth grader by the hip, and pulled his pants down to his ankles. Amid the buzzing of nocturnal insects, Diego and Eduardo listened to the boy sob and plead: "Please don't," he was saying. "No, please." The teacher knelt before the boy's peach-round butt, spread the cheeks with his Kingman hands, and stuck his slobbery tongue, which was the size of a snake, into the blind eye. Diego and Eduardo had to stifle their laughter when they saw the boy piss himself. The teacher smacked his head, and it hung there, leaning to one side, like a hanged man. A few minutes later, after spitting and coating his lover's blind eye with saliva, the teacher made him get down on all fours, grabbed a fistful of dirt with his Kingman hand, smeared it across the boy's damp face, and penetrated him with a single thrust. Diego and Eduardo masturbated to the rhythm of the other man's thrusts, thinking about all the literature they'd been consuming since their rebirth, a body of literature that made them understand themselves and feel surer of what they were doing and what they wanted to do (they wanted to find an Emmanuelle or a Wanda or a Simone or a Juliette; they wanted to be a triangle, a trinity). When the teacher finished with a feral moan into the sixth grader's spread butt cheeks, Diego and Eduardo emerged from the foliage and asked their teacher if they could play with the dirty-faced boy. He smiled, bathed in sweat. "Go ahead," he said. Diego forced the frightened boy to fill his mouth with fallen leaves and suck his penis while Eduardo stuck his fingers up his ass. "It's Basini, it's Basini!" Diego exclaimed when he had the chance to fuck him. The teacher leaned against a tree to watch, stroking his erect cock.

That night Diego and Eduardo went back to their room and fell asleep enjoying the lecherous smell of their seed-coated bodies.

V

Diego was pale as the night, his hair wet with grease.

Eduardo had freckles, vulture eyes, and a head like a hayfield.

Their erect penises were 16.5 centimeters long.

VI

It was easy for them to have sex with girls in higher grades because those girls sought them out with watery expressions and their hands between their legs. The school was strict, much like a prison or mental hospital where the crazy penitents were submitted to a constant process of reformation. Nevertheless, the rules had been made to be broken; fooling the guards and teachers was a challenge that filled the students' days with fun and yearning. That's why Diego and

Eduardo, experts in navigating the surveillance, had effortlessly earned the respect of their classmates. Even the older boys enjoyed their company and applied their methods to evade institutional control. Thanks to them, the art form took over the school like wildfire. Diego was a skilled illustrator of erotic comics, which he exchanged for .avi files of porno movies, and Eduardo was a poet of obscene verses that were imitations of Pietro Aretino, though nobody knew it. *Lustful Sonnets* was part of the budding book collection they'd built by stealing from Diego's dead father's library. Eduardo had learned the following sonnet by heart:

> Stick your finger up my ass, old man,
> Thrust *cazzo* in a little at a time,
> Lift up my leg, maneuver well,
> Now pound with all inhibitions gone.
> I believe this is a tastier feast
> Than eating garlic bread before a fire.
> If you don't like the *potta,* try the back way:
> A real man has got to be a buggerer.
> This time I'll do it in the *potta,*
> But next time in the *cul:* with *cazzo* in *potta* and *cul*
> I feel delight and you are happy and blessed.
> Those who strive to get ahead are crazy,
> They waste their time.
> *Fottere* is the only thing to hanker after.
> Let Sir Courtier croak
> Waiting around for his rival to die.
> I seek only to satisfy my lust.
> (TR. LYNNE LAWNER)

VII

Eduardo and Diego had circulated comics by Milo Manara and Ralf König at school, as well as comic books like *Hessa* (Nazi sadism),

Cicciolina, and others that contained *Belzeba, The Devil's Daughter; The Last Virgin in Paris; The Erotican; Naked for the Bullet; The Impossible Blow Job; White Robes, Dirty Hands; The Forbidden Telenovela; Anal Violence; Preferably a Whore; Latin Lover; Zora the Vampire; The Blond Viper in the Aquarium of Death; Concupiscence; Naga la Maga; Alicia, Professional Call Girl; Only with Your Mouth; The Dress Doesn't Make the Sex; The Truck Driver: Cuckolded and Beat; Orgasms in Brooklyn; Warm Inside; Encyclopenia; Salon for Queens; A Spy Between the Legs; Autosexcomputer;* and an issue of the magazine *Emmanuelle.*

With the money they took from their mothers' wallets every weekend, they were planning to buy *Lost Girls* by Alan Moore and Melinda Gebbie.

VIII

Diego and Eduardo always earned the highest grades in the class. Their natural talent exceeded the expectations of the literature, math, social studies, chemistry, computer science, biology, accounting, English, philosophy, art, religion, and physical education teachers. The literature teacher had such a high opinion of them that she never would have believed, even if someone had told her, that Diego had made her the protagonist in a comic titled *The Digressions of the Succubus Poet* in which he had her sleep with everyone in the grade while writing poetry. The comic had multiple installments and was passed freely around the school in exchange for *Vixen* and *Faster, Pussycat! Kill! Kill!* by Russ Meyer and *Blood Feast* by Herschell G. Lewis.

In the comic's first installment, the succubus poet comes into Diego and Eduardo's classmate Jaime's bedroom window and mounts him while licking his eyes like wells and sticking her tongue in his eye sockets. Jaime's orgasm coincides with screams of pain when the succubus sucks out his eyes like quail eggs and swallows them. Jaime, horrified, moans in the bloody bed while, in the last frames, the succubus pulls a piece of paper from her own ass and uses a blood-soaked finger to write the following lines of Eduardo's: "The eye, tender 'cannibal delicacy' / looks at the eye that squints so as not to be looked at / and sees the blue portrait of its conscience."

In the fifth installment of the comic, the succubus mounts Xavier and forces him to suck her milk-filled breasts until her vagina suddenly reveals hundreds of tiny, sharp teeth and bites her victim's penis, ripping it completely off. Xavier, drugged by the milk, more exhausted than in pain, begs the succubus to give his dick back, and she tells him, her legs spread wide: "Come and get it, if you want." Then Xavier reaches his hands, arms, head, torso, legs in until he's devoured by the vulva constrictor. As her prey explores her bowels, the succubus recites the following lines of Eduardo's: "In the flesh / reason does not exist / intention does not exist / motivations do not exist / only the foreshadowing of vertigo."

In the sixth installment of the comic, the succubus masturbates with a chalkboard eraser while rambling about eroticism and the education system.

IX

In addition to satanic verses, Eduardo wrote pornographic stories that he called exemplary novellas.

X

One Saturday, off school grounds, Diego came up with the idea of hiding a video camera in Eduardo's parents' bedroom. When they watched the video the next morning, they saw nothing but bodies getting dressed or undressed before or after sleeping, bodies that didn't look at each other, like moles digging their own tunnels. They found it sad, but Eduardo was finally able to jack off to the paused image of his mother's breasts: two ostrich eggs that reminded him of too-tall cypress trees, their solitary crowns trembling in a gentle breeze.

XI

Basini jumped off the roof of the main building two months before the school year ended. Against all odds, and to the relief of the PE teacher, he didn't leave a note.

XII

In one of Eduardo's exemplary novellas, the ghost of Osvaldo Lamborghini's proletariat son shows up in a room where his three murderers, all older men, are talking about politics (one of them is running for a city government post). At first it looks like the ghost has come back for revenge, but all he really wants is for one of the three politicians to give him a job. The men, of course, laugh in his non-face and launch into a discussion to persuade the proletariat boy that his existence is essential to their lives because, as a member of the subjugated class, he represents the base of the pyramid that allowed them to sit at the top. Everything shifts when Osvaldo Lamborghini himself enters the room with a notebook and pen and starts writing a new story in which the proletariat boy, despite being a ghost and thus lacking a body, is raped and assaulted again by the three politicians in that very room. However, as he can't be murdered twice, the politicians are forced to give the boy a job. This text transforms reality into its likeness, and in the second story, the three men prostitute the proletariat boy's ghost around the entire Argentine political class. The paragraph that describes the blow job he gives Videla was especially well received by Eduardo's classmates, even those who didn't know who Videla was.

Diego considered *The Proletariat Boy's Ghost* to be the best exemplary novella Eduardo had written; despite its metafictional nature, it proved that above the master and the slave is the writer, right at the top of the pyramid.

XIII

Diego and Eduardo knew they weren't the ones who were writing.

XIV

The dead father's library was full of mysterious hollows; it was composed of books that sunk into the shelves, hiding from intrusive eyes,
and other, cheekier ones that liked to flaunt themselves by sitting a
centimeter or so off the shelf, as if wanting to jump out and open in
midair. Diego always told Eduardo that you should look respectfully
at a library, not as if you were inspecting it (inspection is always a kind
of dissection) but as if you were already familiar with it, as if you
were staring out at a landscape and appreciating the whole, not just
each individual part. Otherwise, he'd say, the library will never show
itself and you'll never see its true face. But it was difficult to see the
books beyond their individuality; it was difficult to see them all as a
single organism, to understand that it does matter that *Psychopathia
Sexualis* by Krafft-Ebing sits next to *Venus in Furs* by Sacher-Masoch
and not *Amatista* by Alicia Steimberg. Eduardo came to grasp the
mysterious unity of the dead father's library whenever he picked
out a book, taking it away forever, because he felt like he'd left the
shelf injured, broken, unstitched in some central place (the paradox
was that all the corners, all the nooks and crannies, were its center),
deformed, even though it had always taken the form of a continuous monster. The violence of this ripping turned him on so much
that he dreamt about black horses galloping over hundreds of forbidden tomes. The eroticism of the perverse sentences made it so that
reading wasn't just a repetition of the laws they'd been taught. To
read well you need to read badly, Diego would say; we have to read
what they don't want us to. Eduardo took this not as irreverence, but
as something essential for freedom. The philosophy teacher had told
them that books would always be subject to censorship because they
have the power to make, remake, unmake the minds of others, but
when Diego and Eduardo asked him about Georges Bataille, he said
it wasn't his area and that, in any case, boys their age weren't ready
for that author's work. If that was so, they thought, the dead father's
library was a mausoleum of disgrace; home to moldy literature that
was more alive than ever, that breathed.

There was something akin to Dr. Frankenstein's work in it—building a library with the remnants of another—but this perspective drew them directly to the line of fire and inoculated them with unknown words.

XV

For Diego and Eduardo, the experience of simultaneously fucking an eleventh-grade girl was staggering; at the same time, it overwhelmed them with mythological images of three-headed beings. Diego penetrated the blind eye and Eduardo the tongueless mouth, the soft, wet mouth with curly hair. It was difficult to coordinate their movements, but she helped them, enthused by the idea of receiving two quasi-men at the same time, of being powerful enough to handle it, of pushing to the extreme her body with its tiny breasts and narrow hips, her almost-woman body that was, in and of itself, still an indistinct project.

"That's why sex is a metaphysical issue," she told them.

XVI

The beginning of the new school year brought Nella, a girl with dark chin-length hair, marble eyes, and the slow, stealthy movements of an abused cat that distrusts all hands.

Diego and Eduardo decided to ignore her.

She reminded them too much of Basini.

Interviewee: El Cuco Martínez

Location: Sor Rita Bar, Carrer de la Mercè, 27, 08002, Barcelona

"I don't know how it happened, tío. We lived in the same fishbowl and were always home at the same time, so we started talking. We'd usually eat together, for one thing. I'd make tortilla de patatas and they'd make Ecuadorian patacones or whatever. At first we talked because that's what we're supposed to do as a species cursed with language. I hate that I can't stand silence when I'm around other people. I wonder what it's about, this need to talk for talking's sake. Although it's actually the most honest function of language, if you think about it. Just saying a word out loud differentiates us from animals. I see you smiling, man, don't take it the wrong way: you're not talking right now, and you don't look like an animal, but that's because your eyes are languagized. What I'm saying is, language transforms us and we're never the same. I dunno. Just look at babies, they're like little monkeys with eyes that could be any mammal's. I don't mean their shape, but what's inside them. Their way of looking. When language touches us—and we touch things with it, naming them, describing them—we think we know everything, understand everything. From then on, it's pure arrogance in our eyes. This poses a problem for knowledge. Programmers know, however, that they don't know a language, they make it. It can take a lifetime to make something, there's a certain working-class humility to it, but knowing implies an absence of movement, it means capturing something like in a photograph and expecting it to never change. I dunno. We should get rid of the phrase 'to know how to talk,' because it suggests that language is already made and there's only one way to learn it. When we say someone doesn't speak properly, it's because we believe there's a correct way of speaking, and tío, doesn't that suck? I like to say that we don't know a language but some of its forms; no one knows how to talk, they just talk, and it's an act that involves a search for and experimentation with grammar and syntax. I'm rambling, so let me try to get back on track: if I say you don't know how to talk, you'll think I'm crazy and don't make any sense. Not a single person in this bar would believe me if I said they don't know how to talk, because everyone is convinced they can, and they confuse being able with knowing how. They don't see language as something that's made and remade, but as a fixed, unchangeable thing. They think truth is beyond words, which only serve to narrate it. That's a problem for knowledge. I dunno. Where was I going with this? OK, fuck it, to say that's what my conversations with the siblings were like early in our friendship. You may not believe me, but we talked about these things. We didn't at first, because we weren't that close, but later we understood each other better. They were literati or whatever you want to call them. They asked me for sci-fi recommendations. I lent them some books."

"So you connected on an intellectual level."

"I dunno, tío. I hate that word. It confuses me. I'd rather say we understood one another. Though that's also a lie."

"Why don't you tell me about Irene, Emilio, and Cecilia. One by one. Tell me about each of them as individuals."

"They don't exist as individuals for me. That sounds awful, I know, but deep down I don't think they liked seeing themselves as separate beings. I think they spent years perfecting the art of seeming like a single person. And it's not that they were alike, because they weren't. Not even physically. I dunno. Irene wasn't afraid to express herself. She was one of those girls who thinks out loud without fearing that people might see her as stupid because she knows full well she isn't. Everything she said seemed like it had come out of a book. The tía talked like she was reading out loud, you know what I mean? She said even the most banal stuff in an unusual way. I liked listening to her, but it could also be awkward, because she could get pretty dark. It wasn't hard to understand her, it's just that she liked getting into subjects that people find really unsettling. I can't think of an example right now. Well, actually I can: child pornography. I get why she'd think about it a lot, but she'd say some really strange stuff, tío; like It's the taboo of our times, and if there's something our societies can't stand it's the sexualization of childhood, and in our generation the transgression of human sexuality must be about sex with children or between children. Then she'd talk about guilt, about children experimenting with their bodies, about the image of childhood she saw as a cultural representation that had nothing to do with the real thing. She'd say children weren't all goodness, tenderness, and innocence, the paradise of orioles and myrtles, but vermin, and they could also be contemptible."

"Right."

"Emilio and Cecilia were more reserved. I dunno. They were intelligent like their sister, but introspective, especially Cecilia, who always spoke in short sentences to show her clipped style. She took tranquilizers. Once she had a pretty rough episode, and the Mexicans got scared because the tía started banging her head against the kitchen wall in a serious way, as if she really wanted to crack her skull. I wasn't there when it happened, but the Mexicans told me they were in their rooms and suddenly, out of the blue, they heard sharp bangs, like a hammer, steady, over and over, at intervals of a second or two, and they thought the sound was coming from the flat next door or upstairs and kept doing their thing, but then when the noise got louder, Kiki went out to see what was going on, because the blows sounded far away and close at the same time, as if they were happening everywhere, and that's when she found Cecilia in the kitchen with her arms hanging limp at the sides of her noodly body, hitting her head against the wall like a sleepwalker. Kiki pushed and hugged her like a straitjacket and yelled for Iván, you know how Mexicans yell, to come help. Irene and Emilio took care of her. The three were very close, maybe too close, I dunno. After a few days the tía got better, and we never had another episode like that."

"But, c'mon, the Teráns must have really trusted you if they asked you to create *Nefando*."

"Well, they needed me. They explained the project, so to speak, and I liked the idea. I didn't know about the videos, because they never told me about them. When I found out, when I saw the videos, the game was almost ready. What interested me was the core idea of *Nefando*. I thought it was awesome. I still do. I already knew about the Deep Web and the Darknet. I still actively explore those layers because I think you can learn a lot from the deep zones. The internet we know is full of places, languages, territories, and it's an alternate world in itself. The strange thing is that, deep down, we don't reinvent anything in this new world. We have this powerful tool, this parallel space that should be ideal, in theory, since it's completely controlled by us, its creators. And yet it has the same functional faults as the physical world—the real one, you might say. All the social problems of our world exist online: theft, pedophilia, pornography, organized crime, drug trafficking, assassinations . . . The only difference is that everyone dares to be criminals or morally wrong, at least once, in the cyber world, but even when we do, we're embarrassed, as if we're incapable of thinking outside the original format. Humans have created this fantastic space of freedom and made it into a carbon copy of the world system. It's as if we weren't creative enough to invent a new moral code that would work online or new representations of ourselves that challenge the ones we've always had."

"So what you're telling me is you thought it was right to put *Nefando* into operation because the internet, for you, should have a different moral code."

"I dunno. Maybe. Tío, I don't know how to talk about this. It was different when I told the police about it. It was easy because I was lying. See? There's always something we don't know how to talk about, something we don't know how to express without saying what we didn't want to say, and yet we think we really know how to talk, even though it's all a total crock of shit, right? Now I know what to tell you, but I don't know how to say it. I have to choose my words, but first I need to think about them and the grammar I'll use to organize them, and it's like building a straw house for the wind to blow away."

"Are you messing with me?"

Irene Terán, age 8. Reader of J. M. Barrie and
H. G. Wells. Drawer of monsters under the bed.
Bedroom with glow-in-the-dark stars.

The father, who had a whitish booger hanging from a hair in his left nostril, threw the daughter into the pool like a sack of rice. She closed her mouth so the water wouldn't burn her insides. She squeezed her face muscles, purplish lips pressed into a raisin, and fell ungracefully but valiantly, or at least that's what she thought she did when she locked the screams in her throat—a yellow canary cage, her mother said—although, deep down, she knew that swallowing the fear was a senseless act of survival and she'd end up opening her mouth just like everyone else. As she sunk into the sky-blue liquid pierced by light casting dense shadows across the large tiles, tiles the size of her head, the daughter thought about the father's booger to distract herself from the fear of dying again. The worst part, she thought, wouldn't be drowning, but that the father would resuscitate her and she'd have to vomit up seas of chlorinated water, only to be thrown into the pool again, like a nightmare within a nightmare, eternally, because the end, she'd come to believe, didn't exist if the father was close enough to bring her back to where she'd left and push her down an unending road. This time, submerged in the golden rectangle of the pool, she didn't kick. Her limbs flopped like a rag doll, and she decided, leaning her head back, to let herself fall, slacken her body, rebel against swimming and against the father's plans. She descended into the sky-blue with her arms and legs splayed like the stars in her bedroom and withstood the burning in her eyes because it's what hurt the least; because the tiles with the shadows and light were a better landscape than the cloud behind her

eyelids. Under the water she could see the sun, the shimmering fig-
ure of the father with his hands on his hips and listen to the watery
laughter that triggered an intense urge to cry. Her body had the
weight of all her toys; her body was like a prism splitting apart the
light it refracts. "Splash, you little bitch!" shouted the father, and this
time she stayed firm in her decision not to. She'd end up drowning
one way or another, but at least this way, motionless, surrendering
to the blue, she didn't feel like the clown of a father that laughed with
a chrysalis booger hanging from his nose. Sometimes the daughter
was surprised by her ability to dissociate when things bored or
scared her. Sinking in the pool, she managed with a little concentra-
tion to remember the famous phrase from *Peter Pan:* "To die will be
an awfully big adventure." And although Mr. Barrie had clearly
written it because he didn't know death is a cyclical scene, a diaphanous refrain, and therefore unexplorable, monotonous, and tor-
turous, those words made her forget the burden of the migratory
pain striking her star body. Her lungs, meanwhile, deflated like two
shriveled balloons, and the water quickly transformed her into an
empty fishbowl. To withstand the fall, she clung to the adventure of
dying a thousand times and to playing the role she'd been given.
When the father filmed her, the daughter would imagine she was
an actress in a romantic movie. The middle son, two centimeters
shorter than her, followed the game so he could bear what happened
when the father closed the curtains. The youngest daughter struggled
to understand her siblings' strategy, though, and she sometimes
cried, and the father laughed so loud that his belly spilled a bit outside his pants and shook like an enormous chunk of Jell-O. From the
sky-blue bottom, she could see that greenish mountain of accumu-
lated fat, a lofty belly that occasionally eclipsed part of the sky. She
couldn't see why the noises of the world, which in those moments
would be reduced to a chain of sullen laughs, entered the water
clearly enough for her to hear them in her descent to the bottom of
the pool. The daughter didn't like the father's laugh: it was an abra-
sive, violating sound, like a rusty bell. The sky-blue distorted the
"Move it, you little whore!" like a mirage, a question: Did the father

want to teach her how to swim or to take revenge for the time he asked her to kiss him and she stuck out her chocolate-stained tongue in a natural reaction of scorn? The daughter wanted to believe the former, and that's why she believed him with an arid conviction that left no room for doubt. Every father wants his daughter to know how to swim. The intention was all that counted; even though the pool afternoons were torture, even though she had nightmares about lizard fish hiding between the tiles, even though she needed first aid a few times, to vomit up clear liquid that burned like napalm, to cough death back into the pool, to be dealt a few blows . . . What mattered was that the motive, the true one, was to save her. The father drowned her so she wouldn't drown; the father opened her mouth with his thumbs and caressed her teeth to give breath back to her; the father laughed to teach her through ridicule. The problem was, no matter how hard she tried, the daughter couldn't formulate or articulate the fog that whirled in a corner of her relationship with the father. There was something contaminating, something intangible or invisible, something she perceived but couldn't say. The situation reminded her of a story she'd read from under the bed in which a bad man believed he was stealing a sample of a virus, but in fact he unintentionally made off with a harmless bacterium that stained its hosts blue. What the bad man had in his hands was hardly helping him attain his goal of getting all of London sick, but in the story, he was sure he was the carrier of a lethal virus. The action in the story was fragmented, disjointed, and the man erred because he believed he was doing something different from what he was actually doing. The daughter sensed she was somewhat like the villain in that story; that there was a version of her life that was unfamiliar to her, a definition of what she was doing, and what the father was doing, that she ignored and that kept her from clearing the fog blocking her view of herself. When she thought too much about what she couldn't say, about everything she didn't know how to articulate, her conviction weakened, and the father's intentions grew darker. But how could she read the intentions of others? How could she know what someone wanted to do when they did something? Did it even matter?

How could you measure the distance between what someone is trying to do and the end result? The daughter tried to consider the
father's reasons for throwing her into a pool for the fourth time in a
row in under an hour; she tried looking beyond what she knew,
beyond the relevance of swimming, and then imagined the father as
a grotesque creature that touched her in all the wrong ways and
made her feel like she was drowning even on dry land. Games
and suppositions aside, it's true that the father threw her into the
pool because this was his intention—it certainly didn't happen by
chance—but his reasons were logical and comprehensible, the daughter thought, like when he shot at the wall of the middle child's bedroom for trying to run away from home and said, aiming the gun at
him, "If I ever shoot you, it's to teach you a lesson." And the middle
son learned. The father couldn't know what the children felt; he
didn't know how it hurt her to sink like an unmanned submarine.
Perhaps swallowing water was the only way to put an end to the fear,
because first you have to fake it so you don't really drown. The problem was that the daughter couldn't identify why the father put her in
front of a camera and insist she tenderly kiss the middle son, or why
he made the youngest daughter crawl on all fours around the living
room floor that was sometimes covered with objects that dug into
her knees. She found the shape of reality mysterious, like a totem of
white masks, and she struggled to make sense of what was happening around her. Lying in those conditions was an accident, an invol-
untary act that happened whenever she opened her mouth. She
didn't mean to deceive anyone, but she lied all the time because it
was easy to distort things when she was underwater and the father
looked like two blobs. How could she believe what she saw with her
half-empty lungs? The mother would never believe her if she didn't
believe herself first. "Swim, you dumb little shit!" the father shouted
as the daughter touched the bottom of the pool. There, where everything was more alive, her hair floated before her like an autonomous
ghost. She tried to swipe it back, but her fingers tangled in the brown
mess, and in this way, tied to herself, missing her hand, she felt a
blind anguish that crept up her heels and made her star position tip

over. She had to unsnarl herself from herself, rip out her hair that only shards of the tile landscape loomed through. Sometimes the mother told her she couldn't understand the things of the world because she was still a little girl. That's why the daughter tried to pull herself out of childhood, just like the father took off her stained clothes to wash her with his fists. She was sure she'd be able to say everything she perceived when she was older, to name it with the right words, make a convincing truth, make some sense of the chaos. She wanted to grow up, wanted her brain to flourish in the noise. She wanted to know why she felt stripped of her identity whenever she was left alone with the father. She'd concluded that adults aren't confused about reality; they all breathe through their mouths to form a solid nest of articulable concepts they use to shape what they see, what they hear, and what they say. The thirty-six-year-old mother always talked with an enviable certainty, and her nest was totally solid. Every time they put on the news, on the radio or television, she looked at the children and told them they were lucky, but the daughter didn't see herself as a lucky person when the father forced her to lick his toes, one by one, and to suck them even though they were dirty and smelled bad. The mother talked about the happiness of the children who had everything, who learned about the world through play, who were loved and protected, and then she left them alone with the father. Once the youngest daughter tried to put into words her disgust with the camera and the calloused hands that touched her under her clothes, but no one listened. Childhood has a quiet voice and an imprecise vocabulary. At school the teacher said you couldn't see every side of a cube from any one position. It bothered the daughter to be a submarine without a periscope. It also hurt her to go without air and lose control of her movements, because, just before she died, her body was independent of her, and when she opened her mouth in a single impulse and the water flooded her throat, stomach, lungs, the only thing that existed was the physical pain shaking her like a puppet, humiliating her, and the noise of thousands of bubbles bursting or ascending, illustrating her desperation while the father cackled outside the pool.

What's the distance between laughter and affliction? Her arms and legs moved on their own, and the daughter looked at them with astonishment as she heard the father's weight crashing into the water like a bomb. Her eyelids closed, but she still had time to ask herself a question: Why did she also want to laugh?

Interviewee: Kiki Ortega

Location: El Gato del Raval, Rambla del Raval, 08001, Barcelona

"Once, a long time ago, I tried to write a story like that."

"Yeah?"

"It doesn't sound real, but I did. I wanted to write about a martyr of empathy, a martyr of understanding, of wanting to put yourself in someone else's shoes, even when they're too small. I couldn't decide whether to make it satire or not. I guess it doesn't matter now that I've lost interest in the subject, but back then I really wanted to do it. I got excited every time I played around with the idea. I was also convinced I could write anything I set my mind to if I just reached into my spiky heart, and I told myself that over and over, quietly, like a prayer. I thought I had a lot to say, that I was full inside, brimming, ready to fill the blank page, but really I was writing to create a language I didn't have. I was tongueless and full of holes. I wanted the words that least belonged to me, the most unfamiliar ones. I wanted to avoid repetition and expand my understanding beyond ready-made phrases. Sometimes you feel the urge to speak, only to realize you don't have anything to say, not even the kernel of an idea, a sad attempt at originality. The story needed a voice, which is why I never wrote it. It was going to be one of those stories we call a novella, or a novella we call a story. In any case, I wanted it to be imprecise, disorienting from the start, because that's how writers are: we like to mess with readers and confuse them and then make sure no one gets lost; or get them lost, sure, so long as they find their way in the end. Deep down we don't care what the reader finds, abandonment, certainty, whatever, they have to find something, or else what was the point to begin with?"

"I see."

"I've always wanted to be both confusing and very clear. That's why my writing is simple and real, tangible and diaphanous: because everything transparent is opaque. What we see is precisely what we never look at. Get it?"

"I think so."

"I wanted to write about a woman whose only purpose in life was to embody the pain of all the women in the world. Not men, mind you: suffering like a man would have been incomprehensible to her. But feeling the pain of other women, at least some of them, would seem like a plausible, appealing goal. I know this means defining pain around gender and sex, but that's what the character was like, and that was the site of the metaphor—the allegory—I wanted to create. My intention was to say that pain isn't transferable or communicable, but the experience of it is: there's a lexicon to describe it, and this lexicon influences how we experience and accept it. I'm too lazy to explain it right . . . In centuries past, menstruating women were forcibly bedridden as if they were sick, and they weren't allowed to do any physical activity. Back then they had to endure menstruation in a way we can't possibly understand today, and they really suffered in their flesh, like a disease, because that's how everyone else described it, and with that language and that monstrous description, that's how they understood it. You see? Pain can be invented, constructed block by block, but that doesn't mean it isn't real. Deep down my character would try to understand the inalienable, however masked by words it might be, and to do so she'd submit to the most brutal experiences. I'm talking about a woman who needs to understand without propositions because she knows pain has no language. I don't know if I'm being clear: the description of the pain is never the description of the pain, is what I mean. The absolute knowledge of such an experience would be unattainable to her, because the simple fact of wanting to feel pain meant that she'd already be distancing herself like crazy from what she was forced to suffer. Her experience, my character's, would be contaminated, but at least she'd come closer to understanding the silence than anyone else. I imagined she'd be interested in the body and not in the mind, or better put, in the mind as a consequence of the body. I was playing around with the idea for months, but I didn't know how to write it. She was an unrealistic character, one who knew that the experience of suffering, like pleasure, is an excess, and excess is connected to corporeality. Because let's not kid ourselves: our bodies are never more ours than when we're in pain. I once wrote an essay for school in which I tried to explain what I felt when I broke my left leg. I was so frustrated that I couldn't convey my pain. I was the only girl in my class who'd broken something, which is why no one knew how much it hurt or how hard it had been not to scream. But I had no words in me. I couldn't convey it. Never in my fucking life had I felt so frustrated. Only imprecise metaphors came to mind, explosions, ripping, burning, and each one of them corresponded to a reality foreign to my experience. Ripping, for example: that's what had happened to me, I'd broken myself, but what does a ripped person feel like? To say I felt a ripping wasn't a way of explaining my pain."

"I've always hated when my doctor asks me to describe how something hurts. I try, but it never comes out right."

"It's tough, güey. That's why she wanted to embody the pain of others, because there's no other way of knowing. I even made a list of the things that would happen in her epistemological research: first she'd inflict all kinds of torture on herself, alone, behind closed doors, for several months, but then she'd go out into the world in search of others to hurt her. She'd get raped, sold, kidnapped, and mutilated. In each sought-after attack, she'd lose part of herself, fall apart, and her language would dissolve to the point of losing her ability to speak and write. She'd be left with nothing but visuals."

"Yeah, but I don't see what all this has to do with my question."

"I think the sleeping woman in *Nefando* was like my character. But that's just my interpretation."

Iván Herrera, age 25. Master in literary creation.

Room #2

It's nighttime. You close the door to your room, running your fingers over your skin as if you've only just met yourself. You're alone and you're pure body, but no one knows that. You can pretend you don't see yourself, hide from yourself, picture yourself as a gentle breeze, an abstraction whose value lies in its absence. Instead, you open your eyes, examine yourself through your clothes, and assume your duality, Quetzalcoatl and Tezcatlipoca, smoking-black-serpent-mirror, part of the oozing sewage mythology where you sometimes shamefully see yourself. It's nighttime. You're alone and split in two. The siblings went out with the Spanish geek, and Kiki is writing an erotic novel in her blind girl's bat cave. You wonder why you've been waiting for this all day, the moment you can lock yourself away and chat with the loathsome-you. You don't often question your desire—you've already dipped into that pit—but your eagerness has you licking your elote teeth and thinking strange things, like when you were still living in CDMX and wandered around La Condesa with your Casper-like tits, and no one knew the truth, not even you. Back then you didn't know yourself, hated yourself in a different way, but now it's nighttime. You're alone. Something within you knows the difference: you need to overwhelm the not-your-body in order to transform and possess it with all its phantasmagoria. You need to not be your face, rip out the markers of artificial identity as if it were a mask gnawing at your head. Luckily, when you get naked, your face gets dark and indistinguishable, a shapeless stain that looks like the parts of your anatomy you cannot see. Sometimes you're blind, Quetzalcoatl. Sometimes you're naked, Tezcatlipoca. You anxiously shed the garments that grace your ungraceful body and let them fall, because they belong beneath you. Now it's only you, the inherited shame, and the well. But beyond that, in a corner of the room, the mirror reflects an ominous, unstable image: your abject *I,* the one who doesn't speak, with its own smoking black mirror you can't look into anymore. Truth is a perverse concept, you explain to the reflection in front of you, just like all those Truths portrayed with a mirror in hand, like yours, Tezcatlipoca; you, too, are welled Truth. You think about Gérôme's series: *Truth at the Bottom of a Well, Truth (Standing) at the Bottom of a Well, Truth Dead at the Bottom of a Well, Truth Coming Out of Her Well to Shame Mankind* . . . This last one makes your serpent Quetzalcoatl stiffen, pointing toward the mirror that undresses you. The nausea rises in your throat, but you swallow it out of habit, cleanliness, solidarity with yourself. Even so, the drop falls from the tip of your phallus, it gets crushed, bursts, and you're suddenly aware of your nakedness, your primate-mammal physiology, "homo" without "sapiens," because of the libido that takes hold of the not-your-body and lifts your flesh in revolt. In that state you can do nothing but stare into the horizon you sink into: Truth with the whip, you confess, makes your belly shake like a blender and forces you to think about your bitch of a mother who never hit you. You would have rather been the child of your friends' mothers, marked by a belt buckle, sobbing under cold water, dealt a sandal slap every once in a while; only then would you have understood in time and accepted your corruption before you grew up. Instead, it's nighttime now: you're alone and withdrawn. Your mommy asked "What's going on, kiddo?" in the syrupy voice of love when all you wanted was for her to beat you. Guilt over what we want is a symptom, ox-hair Emilio once told you. "Of what?" you asked. "Of living in a complex social structure that ties you up by the balls, weirdo," he answered, then started reading a carpentry manual; the cover showed a man with fairy-queen hands wearing a plaid shirt. You would have liked to be one of the Terán sisters so you could fuck Emilio; maybe Irene, the one with the prudish tongue, or Cecilia, the one with the cunning silence. Like cockroaches and compasses, you, too, occur in silence, but you'd rather not brag about that. You walk to the bed without dragging your feet—you refuse to be an invertebrate—and lift the mattress that smells like piss and sweat and pull out a blue box. The body of Gérôme's naked Truth is dressed in grace and yours in shit; your consciousness condemns you to that reality, and you accept it with healthy resignation. The night is clear. On the bedside table you catch sight of the book Kiki lent you: *The Naked Woman,* a novel written in the fifties by Armonía Somers, an Uruguayan woman, one of those books that inexplicably managed to weather contempt and hatred, that tells the story of Rebeca Linke, a woman who gets decapitated on her thirtieth birthday and then sticks her head back onto her body and walks around town, stripped of clothing, to awaken men's dormant desire and violence. You open the blue box and pull out a string as if it were a delicate thread of brown hair. Rebeca Linke's nakedness will never be like the one you now experience in front of the mirror: she isn't a slave to her corporeality, while your shame lies in being a slave to the not-your-body. You'll never be like Rebeca Linke. Thinking about the need to make yourself flesh, you wind a thread around your Quetzalcoatl serpent and pull tight until it turns red and shows its hyena-teeth-veins. The pain clouds your vision for a few seconds, and you close your eyes to protect yourself from the blindness that exists outside you. You feel like you're suffocating a giant worm that creeps out of the deepest, filthiest part of you. You feel disgust and contentment, but the erection persists for a few minutes until the thread starts to dig into your skin and the red you so longed for reveals what you are: organic machinery, maker of an *I* with a plasticine sex. You'd like to hurt yourself so you'll stop thinking with prophet language—as if you knew more about the future than your unmasking—but now you only have the courage to inhale and exhale before wrapping your testicles and clenching your jaw. Rebeca Linke gets naked to be herself, to be reborn in her wounded body. Like you, she wants to free herself: both are beheaded and reconstructed. You pull three needles from the box and carefully lick them. The rhetoric of pain, the psychoanalyst imposed by your beautiful mommy told you in CDMX, is the only tool that will allow you to accept your world so you can live in it without destroying yourself. Dr. Wanker said those kinds of things with a leather agenda on his legs and a wall of diplomas that certified him to listen/speak/think the suffering of others. The process of speaking about pain is painful because it means reformulating the blow, he said, a waxed eyebrow pushing up the skin on his forehead. Dr. Wanker didn't understand anything but thought he understood everything: he believed your mother had beat you, your father had beat you, and that's why even after childhood you'd continued to be a polymorphic pervert. You didn't fit the mold, you weren't diagnosable, you didn't follow the patterns of Freudian theories: you had been a happy child. You plunge the first needle into your Quetzalcoatl serpent. Dr. Wanker fluently recited the same phrases from Lacan and the same poem by Borges. You plunge the second needle in, and your body balks, your hair stands on end, you tear up: you've done it so many times, but now you've made a mistake. Dr. Wanker said he'd met Borges on an airplane and had recited the same poem to him that he launched at you because he believed that was a way to strike up a conversation between equals, between psychoanalyst and poet, and talk about Lacan and Chesterton. You plunge in the third needle and make another mistake: your hand shakes and the blood dances down your member before dripping to the ground. You let out a little scream that could be from pleasure or horror. It's nighttime. You are alone and perforated. The Borges poem ended like this: "I reach my center, my algebra and my key, my mirror. Soon I will know who I am." With a tenuous smile you see the door open and Kiki's black eyes fixed on you, shocked by the blood and nudity.

Soon I'll know who I am. Now I reach my mirror, you think, but she doesn't hear you.

"What the hell, güey! What the fuck did you do, man? I'm calling an ambulance right now. Come on! That's fucked up!"

Interviewee: El Cuco Martínez

Location: Sor Rita Bar, Carrer de la Mercè, 27, 08002, Barcelona

"I don't know what you think my relationship with the Teráns was like, but I'll tell you that whatever story you're putting together in your head, the truth is going to disappoint you. It's true, I won't deny it, we spent a lot of time together, but that doesn't mean they told me everything or that we were like a family. In fact, we always maintained a basic distance that helped us skirt the pitfalls of living together. We'd talk in the living room at night, and since we lived together, of course they knew I was good with computers and all that shit. But I dunno, I really don't know. The first time they told me about *Nefando*, and this is what I remember, they mentioned it as if it were just another of their many projects, the kind they didn't have any intention of actually going through with, you know: They talked big, like most people. Bah, like everyone. You couldn't tell when they were serious. They didn't go into much detail, and I remember telling them it seemed like an interesting idea, but a strange one. Yes, it was a strange idea for a video game. Then my curiosity was piqued, and I asked them to tell me everything they'd thought up, and tío, I lost my mind. When they said they were seriously working on the project, that they were really going to do it, I told them: I'm here, kids, I can do it. I can make what you want."

"But you told me the Teráns had asked you to help, not that you'd offered to create the game for them."

"Tío, come on, it's clearer than water that if I hadn't offered, they would've asked me to lend a hand. The three of them, Irene, Emilio, and Cecilia Terán, knew I'd taken video game design courses. They knew I was a hacker. They knew I was in the demoscene world . . .

They didn't have a fucking clue about computers and needed some-one like me. I don't mean to brag, but it's hard to find someone who can put everything into a video game for you, do it totally for free, and be discreet. Without me, *Nefando* wouldn't have existed. The Teráns knew perfectly well what they were doing when they told me about the project. They were hoping I'd offer to help, and I did."

"Got it."

"What I'll never be able to understand is how such a huge mess came out of a video game, a representation of the shit that's all around us every day, a simple staging of what's impossible to look at: the backs of our own necks. But no, now it turns out it's reprehen-sible to make shit playful. Shit can only be shit, they tell us, so shut up. Shit must cause revulsion, not amusement. But *Nefando* caused revulsion, yes. Did it ever! I can tell you that much. I suppose we're all attracted to what disgusts us and want to scare ourselves, even though we don't like to admit that fear is pleasurable. We're complex creatures, that's for sure."

"I'm sorry to contradict you, but the videos in that game weren't representations. They were real recordings."

"I don't see the difference. I don't think there's anything realer in this fucking world than our representations of it. Sometimes we end up talking in metaphors when we're speaking most frankly. Haven't you noticed?"

"No, and don't change the subject. This is a separate issue."

"You're so funny, tío. Really, you're incredible."

Kiki Ortega, age 23. FONCA scholar.

Room #1

She opened the door and walked to the living room, sweeping the floor with her toes. *I have broom-toes and a broom-soul and a broom-mind, she thought, I'm like fucking María la del Barrio when I should be saving my energy, lying on a beautiful pebble beach, and protecting my words: they're all I have.* El Cuco was sprawled out on the sofa with his face smashed, coat shredded, dirty backpack empty, hands like earthquakes, muttering insults as Irene wiped his split lip with a kitchen towel. *To write is to give meaning to my sweeper discourse, you assholes, why do you pull me from my writing that is my cleaning?* At his side, Emilio watched as if blood roses bloomed from his left cheek, a well-tended garden of violence, but El Cuco didn't notice because one eye was cocooned and the other stared skyward. Cecilia and Iván watched everything from a safe distance, a puddle-dodging-distance, a distance you keep from an accident when no one knows the injured person. They beat you up good, güey, what happened? Iván asked. Some fucking Muslims, he said, robbed me, he said, they took everything, he said. *The first thing these Spanish douchebags come up with is racist bullshit.* They robbed you? Yes, dammit! Relax, relax, buddy. Are you going to report it? El Cuco seized the moment when Irene dropped the towel with dancing lobsters onto the table to stand up, pick up his backpack, walk past Cecilia, who was scratching her nose, and go to his room. I bet he won't report it, Iván said once the door had slammed. *Thieves don't report other thieves, but I can't say this out loud: I should keep my mouth shut about this.* What do we do? Cecilia asked. No one was looking at the red towel on the table except for Kiki. He'll be all right, Irene said, it isn't serious.

What's serious is that no one's going to wash the kitchen towel, and it's going to just sit there stained with the bodily fluids of an idiot who doesn't give a shit his face was destroyed. I didn't think these things actually happened here, because it's the first world and everyone's happy, Iván said. Cecilia walked down the hall, a shadow shrinking onto the wall. Are they happy? *This apartment is a dump and I don't have time to deal with it, because I have to write and bathe myself and save my energy so I can lie on a beach with wet stones.* They're happy, right? Iván insisted. Irene smiled, and two bowls were carved out in her amber-rose Rubén Darío cheeks. *To lie down on a pile of stones soaked by the drool of God.* Someone should put that in the washing machine, Emilio said, pointing at the stained cloth on the table. *It's for the best they don't have voices: not Eduardo, not Diego, not Nella. It's better they don't say anything.*

She returned to her lair to avoid the laundry debate—Irene would say her back hurt, that it felt like her spine was sunsetted or guillotined, and no one would understand what she was saying, just her diluvial antelope-face hoping its horns would be kissed before the sacrifice. *It is impossible to write a pornographic novel that isn't a pastiche or a cynical, ironic text that mocks its own fears.* Inside she had to push the swollen wood of the door repeatedly for it to close its jaws. Everything became vast in the heat; that's why July afternoon streets were hostile carriers of diseases like blindness from oversaturation, muteness from unvocalized reasoning, deafness from an accumulation of falsetto noises, numbness in the skin and eyes and heart— the mythological muscle that simplifies all narratives. *What's written here has to be more important than silence, she thought.* Sometimes it was as if she were playing an emblematic character: Jonas in the whale or rather Jonas in the crocodile-room, being digested by an enormous ulcered stomach. *The question is: How do you make a pornography of love?* On the table rested a Faber-Castell pencil with its yellow body gnawed and peeled. Many years ago, Gladys, the one with the soft hands, pink bow, and Barney backpack, buried a pencil just above her right knee in the middle of a grammar lesson. *Eroticism is violent, like nature.* She did it voluntarily, little Gladys, because she'd fought with a boy whose hair fell across his forehead, and she wanted to pull him all the way down into the bottom of the pit, which was, at the time—and always will be—rejection. *There is no eroticism that denies horror.* She remembered how Gladys had stood up as if nothing had happened, with her spotless uniform and new wound, and walked up to the teacher to tell him that the mushroom-headed boy with butterfly eyelashes had stabbed the yellow pencil into her leg. *Desire is like hundreds of birds crashing into a closed mouth.* She pointed at him, repeatedly drawing a smile in the elementary school air with her index finger, and blamed him without crying, her face white or maybe not, perhaps paved with childish hatred. *Horror and desire embrace underwater and forget to breathe.* Her friendship with sweet Gladys ended forever that morning. *Horror and desire die, drown, know how to laugh.* Though sometimes Kiki thought about her when writing at night, and it was as if the landscape filled with dikes and dunes and perfectly aligned niches. *Desire outlasts terror through laughter.* Sometimes when Kiki thought about Gladys, she understood people. *Horror is demystified through laughter.* She also understood the blank page, the virtual silence, even the mute world if she thought about Gladys's accusatory face. *Horror and desire have the same face sculpted in the skies.* Why write and not go out and play, run, fuck? *It's necessary to pornographize life in order to say what the insistent coating-cradle-of-all-cultures didn't dare utter.* Writing was her way of pointing her finger. *It's impossible to novelize the collapse through the theology of clothing.* It was her way of hurting herself and blaming others for her verbal lesions. *The problem is no one knows how to say what has never been said.* She sat on the bed and thought about some decrepit writer's column that Iván had emailed her. *The limits of language are our chasms.* The writer cited the note written by one of the Kursk crew members, the men on the submarine that now rests on the bottom of the ocean, *There one lies at ease:* "13:15. All personnel from section six, seven, and eight have moved to section nine, twenty-three people are here. We have made the decision as a result of the accident. None of us can get out. I am writing blind." The writer—in his decrepit column—considered the literary quality of those sentences and concluded that literature springs from necessity and that the writer—the crew member—was the one who, spattered with fear, felt the urge to describe what was happening around him. *Revulsion is worth articulating; someone needs to get dirty in language so others can see themselves.* She, however, thought that talking about literature in a note about a man just before his death was reductive and cowardly. *There are empires of fireflies in the unnamable.* Or perhaps it bothered her that she didn't know what to say. *I am writing blind, she thought, I feel compelled to say what I don't know how to say.* A pornographic language could be the one that reveals the word, the one that could rip her out of her robes and violate her normativity. *I am writing blind.* But maybe that goal was too ambitious; an area she couldn't access because the desperation still hadn't turned her into a crew member on the Kursk or a Chilean miner who broke grammar by writing "We are OK in the refuge, the 33." *The moving word of desire, the word that excites the body pretending to be flawless, the word filthy with the private made public, the word that tastes like ceremony.* She still didn't break her language, and that's why an unfamiliar order, like a clear tide pool next to the sea, kept her from thinking and writing from Gladys's perspective: the clarity, the psychology of the human. *What am I but digested flesh in confinement?* Pornography only existed in the retinas of morality: it was the negated truth.

Irene pushed the door open and came in, stepping on her life that was digested flesh in confinement.

"Hey, Kiko," she said, lighting a pipe, "wanna play a game?"

Interviewee: Iván Herrera

Location: Starbucks, Col. Hipódromo Condesa, 06100, Mexico City

". . . Because the truth is I never found out. I never asked, and I don't regret it. We both volunteered to test it, but the two of us never talked about the experience with each other, only with the Teráns. There was no avoiding them. They wanted to know what we thought, how we reacted when we played. That's why they got us involved, if you must know."

"And what did you think of it?"

"It was fucking horseshit."

"Could you be more descriptive?"

"Well, it was a game you didn't really play."

"I don't understand."

"It's too fucking complicated to explain. I'm not even sure you can call something a game if it isn't entertaining. *Nefando* got its players hooked not because it was fun but because it managed to awaken a certain curiosity . . . How can I put it? A morbid curiosity that swells inside, you know? Like a stain throbbing in your belly button. After a little while you'd end up looking like a zebra, but with wider black stripes than normal, covering your lamb-white soul. It was as if your skin were covered in scythes, and by the time you noticed, you were already all cut up and blackened. Well anyway, putting this bullshit aside, what I can tell you is there weren't any rules, obstacles to overcome, or levels . . . All you did in *Nefando* was watch and wait without knowing what for. You could say it was a game for voyeurs because you went around checking and clicking on things and that's how you learned, or didn't, what was going on, though it was always nothing in the end, at least at first. The nothing was happening at all times, on a loop, because *Nefando* wasn't made to please anyone but its creators. That's why I say it wasn't a game, though it pretended to be one: because it transcended all known genres and situated itself in a sort of limbo of imposture. Like I said, *Nefando* went against the unwritten rule that says games should be recreational. You didn't play this one: you read, you searched, you spied, you feared. Several times I thought: If I disappear, this will go on without me. I felt expendable in the game. I felt like a blown-out candle, totally useless. You might think I'm crazy, but it was as if the game played you, not the other way around. Give me time to explain, let's see if I can brush off the dirt I've just thrown on top: I'd never played a video game in which more than three hours passed without anything happening, but that still kept me glued to the chair, watching that dense, inhospitable nothing that looked like my own nothingness. Maybe the players, just like me, just like Kiki, did it because they discovered the nothing encrusted between their eyebrows and could no longer do anything but accept it and sink into the pit of the screen."

"It's impossible that nothing happened in the game."

"No, well, things did happen, but deep down nothing did, get it? *Nefando* was an online game that didn't define itself. An important part of the experience was discovering what the game was about. That was striking too: the search for what it meant. When I played, I felt the need to find some meaning there. I thought it must have one."

"And did it?"

"I don't know. Maybe many, maybe none. Did Kiki tell you about her experience?"

"No."

"That's a shame, güey. I would've liked to know."

"I understand Kiki was working as a translator at the time."

"Yeah, but she wasn't translating novels or anything literary."

"No?"

"Nope. She translated texts for a website on Maya healing."

"Was she translating them from Nahuatl or what?"

"No, güey, Nahuatl is an Aztec language. K'iche' is a Mayan language, as is Tseltal, Ixil, Akateko, or Poqomam. Plus the healing course wasn't Maya-Maya, but Western Maya, Maya for first-worlders looking for exotic cures for their spirits. The Mexicans don't have a fucking clue what Maya healing is, just like the Mayas wouldn't know either. So she translated the texts from Spanish to French and English. It was esoteric bullshit. Kiki showed me the website once. It said the course objectives were to get outside your comfort zone, explore unknown territories, awaken your consciousness, identify imaginary assets, acquire knowledge of the holographic star package, co-create with God and not with the devil, caress the chalice of knowledge, and other shit like that. They invited you to pay by asking if you'd like to know the three universal principles handed down by Maya knowledge so you could take the reins of your life. It was virtual pre-Columbian self-help."

"Ah."

"I wish I knew what that chick's experience with *Nefando* was like. We were too depressed to ask each other back then, but now I want to know."

"I have a question I'm going to ask only you: Why do you think the Teráns created *Nefando*? What do you think they wanted to do with it?"

"Nothing. That's the answer. Why do we create things? Why do we talk and make babies and write and compose and paint? For nothing and for everything. The end goal is creation itself: they created *Nefando* to create *Nefando*. Or do you think they didn't know the game would eventually be taken down? The Teráns knew, as everyone knows, that it's a crime to upload that kind of video, but they didn't give a shit. They wanted to express themselves, I guess, kill some time, fuck things up, what do I know. Kiki wrote a novel and they invented a video game. Everyone does their own thing."

"ok, let's change the subject. The siblings had scholarships from the University of Barcelona, but they never went to class."

"Yeah, they lost the scholarship because they didn't go."

"And do know how they supported themselves?"

"I know now."

"Oh yeah? And what do you know?"

"First tell me one thing, güey: What's all that you're writing?"

El Cuco Martínez, age 29. Hacker. Scener. Video game designer.

Room #3

They turned off the lights and the auditorium erased its four walls, first becoming a humpback whale's brain and then the limp body of a jellyfish, letting off sparks of electricity on little screens, on dozens of lenses, on their fish eyes, until the ocean pulled back, leaving only people and computers and the blue image on a foamy white wall, applause, and the beginning of a 4 kB intro that showed cubes becoming spheres on a vast lake of fire. During the presentation, El Cuco turned his chair toward Irene, Cecilia, and Emilio, who were looking straight ahead with buzzing eyes, and he wondered how much they understood, even though that was irrelevant because they were there, with their hands limp on their knees, their lips rusty, carried away by an equestrian curiosity galloping across their tongues, bellies, backs, so that later—when they left the unwalled room—they could say they'd attended a demoparty: a show for geeks with hair that was too short or too long, т-shirts featuring the Atari logo, and flaccid bodies that could have been dreamt up by some science fiction prophet. They'd also brag about having seen moving images created by a language they didn't know, breathed among fifty sceners, heard the frenetic typing of stinger-like crooked fingers and the tumbling of hundreds of pebbles onto a plastic surface or, as Irene put it, the collapse of the typewriter's alphabet. The Teráns had made friends and discussed science fiction novels like *Neuromancer* and the human dichotomy, repeated in many literary works, of mind and body as opposing forces, the repulsion of the meat,

/ /Henry Dorsett Case says to himself: "It's the meat
talking, ignore it,"
Irene said,
and she also said: The desire for virtuality,
to make it the intended reality,
is nothing but the longing to leave the bodily prison.

spilling the *I* from the bottle: The monster created by Victor
Frankenstein, Emilio said, is horrifying because everyone sees it as
pure flesh without language. But the monster does talk, corrected
Jordi, a scener and taxidermy enthusiast. Yeah, yeah, he responded,
but no one hears him, his language doesn't exist for others, and his
voice is inaudible, people see him as a creature without subjectivity because he comes alive in what gets gnawed away, because he's
incapable of being beyond his body. El Cuco crossed his arms: The
best works of science fiction are situated in dystopias where nature
has been destroyed and replaced with high technology. The body
reminds us we're dirt, Jordi said, but nature scares us, so we hide
from it. Cecilia, with her glasses and long nails, El Cuco thought
from his seat, looked like the incarnation of Molly Millions, body-
guard and lover of Case, a cyborg girl who overcame her physical
limitations with electronic prostheses, a femme fatale in a bicepha-
lous world, even though most of the time he saw the siblings as a
single person, an inhabitant of Gethen, the planet of hermaphrodites
invented by Ursula K. Le Guin,

/ /Sometimes I am Emilio and sometimes I am Cecilia,
Irene said,
and she also said: But almost never am I me.

beings without a definite sexual identity who existed bubbling outside the binary. The siblings were indistinguishable to him because
they had the same frosty, thrashed face inside. I'm afraid of the fragility of my body, Irene once confessed, but my mind, even though
it breaks, is as tough as a flowering cactus. Shit, tía, you sure have a

way with words, El Cuco blurted out mockingly. The Teráns were the same: their eyes were a gloomy green, their skin like a kiwi's. They fixed their forest-like irises on an intro that showed a path zigzagging into a machine. The soundtrack was a dubstep that ricocheted over El Cuco's eardrums as if birds were squawking in his bones. When are they putting yours on? Cecilia asked, and he said soon. One of the most childish speeches in science fiction comes from John Galt in *Atlas Shrugged,* Jordi said. Why childish? Emilio asked. Because of its intellectual elitism, he answered. I agree, it's true, Emilio said, it's also a neoliberal fable. Who is John Galt? everyone in the novel wonders until Galt turns up and delivers a speech that El Cuco only half-remembered but had once found compelling, back when he left his mother with obsessive-compulsive disorder alone in Madrid and moved to Barcelona and decided not to contact her again.

/ /John Galt says NO to sacrifice,
Cecilia said,
and she also said: People who don't know anything about
philosophy think
it's a philosophical novel,
when it's really the tantrum of a rich girl
who doesn't like the syntagma "social responsibility."

/ /John Galt is Ayn Rand's true alter ego,
Irene said.

El Cuco had seen his mother the year before, when the television program *Hay una cosa que te quiero decir* showed up and asked, shoving a camera in his face, if he'd consider coming to the set so he could meet someone who wanted to tell him something. Why doesn't this person come and talk to me here? he asked the girl with the Cheshire Cat smile. Because sometimes it's easier to find the courage if there's an intermediary, she answered into the camera as if he didn't exist. I don't think I'll go, he concluded. Why not? she asked, feigning curiosity. Because, no offense, but your program uses people's private lives to put on a show and make everyone think it's cool to turn someone's actual problems into a theme park, he answered. The girl smoothed an eyebrow with her thumb and asked if he wanted payment in exchange for his participation. Man, it would be stupid not to accept, the cameraman said, and El Cuco accepted. They brought him to the studio, put a little makeup on, placed some apparatuses under his clothes, and made him walk through a brightly lit tunnel onto a blue-and-white stage with a bench where he could sit and wait. The host, with a ceremonial smirk, told him there was someone who wanted to tell him something and asked if he had any idea who it was. El Cuco said yes: his mother. The audience applauded like a group of trained walruses. There was a screen in front of him that looked like an envelope, and when it was opened, to his surprise, he didn't see his mother there, but his ex-girlfriend Lola. Lola has been living with a friend for two years and is now an independent woman, the host said. She knows you don't get along with her family, that you don't like her father's bullying personality, and that, deep down, you don't like hers either. So, with a lot of courage, with a lot of gusto, she left the nest, flapped her wings, flew away, and never looked back. Right, El Cuco answered, thinking about how to get out of this mess. Now she's here, looking for you, to tell you she's changed, that she's got a job and goes to school and her parents don't run her life, the host said, tottering around the stage like a penguin. Lola has taken the reins and wants to let you know, to confess her love, to tell you she forgives your kleptomania and she's determined to start over. Is there anything you'd like to tell her?

/ /The lights were absolute and made no space
for the shadow growing over El Cuco from behind his ears.

What we had is no longer possible, he told Lola, because he'd heard it somewhere and because it was the first thing that came to mind. The walruses stopped clapping, and the silence was like hundreds of crickets jumping all over your face, but he managed to simulate a rusty, sputtering inner peace that convinced the audience, according to the person who removed the apparatus from under his clothes after the curtain dropped. Later, when they gave him the money and let him go, he walked around Madrid, not understanding why his feet led him to the place he knew his mother would be. He looked at her as if that meant something, as if finding her was a good deed. She was next to the bear and strawberry tree in Puerta del Sol, with her head down, burying her chin in her chest, the way she sat every night, but El Cuco didn't come closer because he wasn't ready to sacrifice himself. He wanted to be happy. So he left.

/ /Philip K. Dick, Philip K. Dick, Philip K. Dick,
Cecilia said,
and she also said: I like the sound of Philip K. Dick,
Philip K. Dick, Philip K. Dick, Philip K. Dick.

They're about to put your intro on! Irene said with a blooming smile that made him think of ferns and rocky places stretching out under the sun. He looked up at the image projected on the wall and saw the title of his work, *Factor Kipple,* with a pride he wanted to trounce and disappear. What does it mean? Emilio asked. *Kipple* is a term that appears in *Do Androids Dream of Electric Sheep?* to designate everything that's useless, that has no practical function and only takes up space, he answered. We live in a kippleized world, Cecilia said. No, not entirely, El Cuco said, we'd have to abandon the planet for that, like in the novel. Shhh, it's about to start, Emilio said.

/ /Kippleized world or trash can or fire on brown junk that says:
God exists or nothing exists.
And we all regurgitate: Nothing.

They looked at the illuminated wall. In the darkness, their hair looked like spiders on warm heads, more transfigured than ever, and El Cuco thought it didn't matter how much intelligence was housed in those heads, behind those fly eyes watching his intro flung like a gob of spit onto the haunches of a wall, because no one would understand from his trash-world images what he'd been thinking while writing the code. At the same time, it was only what he'd thought deserved to be seen with the same attention that gleamed onto the planetary face of everyone's cheeks and parted lips. They wouldn't know that: they wouldn't see that he'd thought about desire, mobile from his *I*, reflected on a screen; about his need to fill the empty spaces with specters; about the ambiguity of his skin; and about the only unrepresentable constant: chaos. His desire for nothing was drawn on the metallic rubble that formed the landscape of *Factor Kipple*. Let's create a theory of trash, Irene whispered in his ear, let's say we reveal ourselves in it. No, El Cuco answered, we never see ourselves in what we throw out. Do you see yourself in your own body or in that, she asked, pointing at the images of his projected intro, what you throw away? El Cuco suddenly looked at her as if she contained the possibility of a pleasure he wouldn't have to be ashamed of, a native, latent pleasure steeped with wind, but the moment fell apart when Irene moved away, and he knew she was just as fleeting as her own voice. We want to show you a necrozoophilia forum we found navigating the deep throat, Emilio told him when someone else's intro started. What? El Cuco asked. On the Deep Web, he clarified. You have no idea what we've been reading! Cecilia told him, We could write a better novel than Kiki's,

/ /I don't know my trash, El Cuco thought,
and he also thought: But I will be resurrected in it.

starting with the stories that go viral in the forums. To narrate our horrors, what's the point of science if not to narrate our horrors? El Cuco thought, What's the point of technology if not to narrate our horrors? What's the point of languages, screams, keyboards, wells if not to narrate our horrors? The desire to say "desire" isn't alleviated by speaking, Emilio once told him, sometimes we have to act and allow what's done to articulate our vertigo. We need you to create *Nefando,* Irene told him with a thin smile. The auditorium lights came on.

Interviewee: Kiki Ortega

Location: El Gato del Raval, Rambla del Raval, 08001, Barcelona

"But I didn't know they had a website for that kind of thing, much less that they were making money off it."

"I see."

"All Iván and I knew, because we lived with them and it would have been impossible not to notice, was that they spent a fuck-ton of hours a day scanning books they brought home. They'd borrow them from the public libraries—which in my opinion is the best thing this city has going for it—and come home with their backpacks full of poetry collections, novels, essays, comic books . . . Sometimes they'd also steal books from Fnac, but that wasn't really their style. What I mean is that it was quite unusual for them to get into trouble. I'm sure of it. In any case they were doing brave, legitimate work. Don't look at me like that, güey, I know what's going through your head. There are people who can't afford to buy a book or a movie ticket, but this high and mighty society thinks it's morally wrong that piracy makes cultural products available for free. Fucking assholes, güey. Fucking slave world. Supposedly it's taboo to talk about this stuff because it implies the negation of the legal system, the pornography of the market, but I don't give a fuck what defenders of intellectual property say, because, of course, they defend the inanest concept ever invented. Because copyrighting ideas and artistic creations is a repulsive kind of elitism, truth be told. I'm not saying we should deny authorship to authors, but we should think about what piracy does for the people. The siblings once told me that filmmakers in Ecuador make a deal with the pirated-DVD sellers to pirate their movies, and that's super cool, right, because the world is horribly unequal and we, the third-world simpletons, know that better than anyone. I write and hope I'll be able to publish someday, but not because I want to make a show of my intellectual property or restrict the circulation of whatever I make to the little group of people who can pay for it. I want to publish because when an editor takes a risk on your work, others are more likely to read you, and I write to be read, dude, not to go around playing the part of the tortured writer-type. In fact, I'd love if someone pirated my work once it's published. The day I'm pirated I'll celebrate for real, I swear."

"OK."

"And it's not like I'm against people who can just go to the store whenever they want and put their money on the table. I buy the books I want to read, when I can, and I rent movies. I'm only trying to say that reality is thorny, right? And that those who can't afford to pay for an original product, whether that's because the system screws them over or because they struggle to feed themselves every month, also have the right to read and go to the movies. I think artists should come down from their ivory tower and get socially involved."

"Artists also have to eat."

"Well, they should work, güey! They should get their little porcelain hands dirty like the rest of the mortals in the working world. They're asshole sons of bitches who think—what morons—that just because they make art, their human condition is superior to everyone else's. Miserable assholes. And neither the artists nor the cultural market will sink because of the people who post links to download books, movies, or TV series. Companies make less than before, but they're still making money. When a business goes under, it's because it can't adapt to the new circumstances of the game or because it refuses to lower its prices."

"Then you didn't know the Teráns had created a website called Proyecto Cratos where they stored links for free downloads."

"No, güey. I already told you I didn't."

"Then you also don't know if they were the ones who sold ad space, or if it was El Cuco who created the page, or if . . ."

"No."

"You also don't know if they sold the website."

"No."

"I frankly find it strange you didn't know anything about Proyecto Cratos when you did know about *Nefando*."

"Well, they're two completely different things. First off, *Nefando* didn't make the siblings a single euro."

"I also find it strange that El Cuco admitted he'd created *Nefando*, but he also swears he didn't know anything about Proyecto Cratos."

"I don't see any reason for him to lie."

"Are you lying?"

"Like everyone else, dude."

The Hype Pornovela Library

CHAPTER TWO
By Kiki Ortega

I

Beneath a cold violet dawn, Diego and Eduardo quickly mastered how to use their tongues to pick up the taste of the most sinuous parts of their wet caravel bodies. They learned their tongues were wingless trophies, forces that dragged fish and serpents from empty pits and explored, without a headlamp, the salivated curves of a skin so white it was dark, mixed, and wooded. They also learned that in some places birds die impaled on their own songs—sometimes round, sometimes fine-speared—and that pleasure is a mole that digs through the red moans of its blood toward a thin light forbidden by an austere order and intensified by the civility of language.

Some nights they sang:

> "The navel of the world's thirst was their skin:
> The navel of the world's skin was their thirst."

Some nights they quickly masturbated.

II

Diego and Eduardo delightedly read the graphic novel by Alan Moore and Melinda Gebbie, *Lost Girls,* in which Dorothy, Alice, and Wendy, protagonists of the children's classics *The Wizard of Oz, Alice in*

Wonderland, and *Peter Pan,* meet as adults in a luxury hotel at the beginning of World War I. Accompanied by a horse in heat, a rapist rabbit, and a sodomitic Hook, the three slip down a spiral of erotic narratives that reveal new interpretations of their pasts and inspire them to wind the broken clocks of their repressed sexualities.

Eduardo liked that the comic referenced the Marquis de Sade, Pierre Louÿs, and Oscar Wilde.

Diego admired the narrative decision to have pleasure be invaded by war, death, and a red poppy.

III

To Eduardo, Nella was a fish of stagnant water: innocuous, gray, and woven in shadows.

To Diego, she was a brown insect to be crowned by the sole of his shoe.

IV

In one of his exemplary novellas, one of the shortest and most poetic, Eduardo dared to change the ending of Griselda Gambaro's *The Impenetrable Madam X;* a toothless work collapsed onto a bed of violet cackles he found hidden among dust and tremors, arteries and yellowing pages, on the left-hand side of the dead father's library—a region of simultaneous hell and paradise—and read during a few math classes. Even though Gambaro hadn't let her characters make each other tremble, so the agreed-upon seisms in the letters they write to each other are never realized, so they barely squeeze hands; even though she kills Jonathan in front of his beloved Madam X and condemns them both to frustration, fear of hunger, fingers down the throat (though the former is saved by death and the second overwhelmed by life); even though she'd allowed Madam X to surrender and let herself fall—with the putrefaction of her love on the tip of her tongue—into the plump arms of Marie, the servant who likes to touch and lick her, Eduardo, the boy who does the rewriting, disrupts the final message of the novel by eroticizing death and erasing surrender. In his little story, Madam X enjoys Jonathan's rigor mortis so that, in the end, she can satisfy her winged desire and violate the novel's opening sentence: "The greatest obstacle facing the erotic novel is its struggle to reach literary climax."

"Jonathan's hard, still-warm body on the rug made her lift her dress," Eduardo wrote, "extract the enormous member from its cage, and stick it deep inside her. She screamed as if she were about to faint: the dead thing felt like a sun illuminating her belly."

"Make it so she also sticks it up her ass," Diego suggested.

"The dead thing was like a sun illuminating her rectum."

V

The classes, boarding school, and teachers all convinced Diego and Eduardo that there was something inside a human being that couldn't be educated, something that seethed and wasn't subject to the cords, something that beat tumultuously, like an inner bell whose resonance is destined to alter what has been established in them. It was a primitive part, existing beyond language, only interested in its own wild, violent condition, in responding to stimuli, in not depriving itself of anything or anyone, and it called them, like it does everyone, with an inane force.

That part, unbraided and submerged, expanded in their bowels when, as they railed a tenth-grade girl in an empty classroom, Nella, the gray fish, the brown insect, came in as if nothing were going on, collected her history book, and left without daring to look them in the eyes.

VI

Diego and Eduardo knew a satisfied sexuality inevitably leads to death.

That's why they so enjoyed their thirst, navel of the world.

VII

Nella came to school walking through walls, like a ghost, without anyone noticing her tenuous existence, her insolent gait, or her smile shaped like a broken fan. Before the teachers could ask that she introduce herself, she'd managed to blend into the scenery and simulate her own absence, making herself transparent, holding a stiff, upright posture, breathing like a plant. Diego and Eduardo were irritated by her insect or freshwater-fish personality, her opaline voice, watery eyes, black chin-length hair, her neck like a narrow, clean canal, but ever since the day she caught them fucking Julia Grande in the classroom, they unwittingly started watching her with unusual angst. Then they noticed her self-elected specter condition, her milky face, and thick wet lips like a pair of little worms. Nella, they concluded with the sharpness of amateur detectives, seemed comfortable in her solitude, distanced from the other girls in class, uninterested in anything but her anatomy books— she even read them during class—or the camera she hung around her neck to hunt cats at recess. On several occasions, they saw her go into the forest and let off flashes, chasing some animal or disappearing just because, because she didn't like to be chased and wanted to curl up shackled by a false freedom. She was the only girl who voluntarily didn't interact with anybody; the only one who slipped her hand under her skirt every time she answered a teacher's question; the only one who didn't sing or close her legs when she sat down; the only one who'd never dared look them in the eyes but who didn't seem intimidated, either, when she noticed their scornful scrutiny.

They hated her as if they knew they'd love her.

VIII

In one of her digressions, the succubus poet masturbates with a chalkboard eraser while constructing the following monologue: "Dear teacher: Every day I learn to unlearn myself, to stray from your footsteps, because I prefer saliva, the smell of weeks and blood, over the book that says 'My body emptied of rivers, my body dried of waves.' The pages you read to me emptied my rivers and dried my waves; they repeated my nonexistent hole. I don't want the education you try to teach me to see. I swallowed five pairs of eyes so I'd view the world as a pentagon, that is, complete and enormous according to the history of geometry. That's how I know how to look at my sex made up of five absolute forms, all broken and pierced by pins and white feathers, that's why I learn to unlearn myself, to go (back) over myself, to erase what I was taught about control and incest and the screams and the bites of the morally wounded hyenas. I wasn't taught how to love here, teacher. I'm sad, very sad. I wasn't taught how to love."

IX

"I don't want anything that pulls me away from life," Eduardo wrote, "but what brings me closer to it is what drags me toward death."

X

Diego and Eduardo took advantage of a hot, cricket-filled night to go skinny-dipping in the lake. They dove in open-eyed, listening to the silence impregnated with the noise of life, a murmur populated with monotonous, drawn-out buzzing; splashing, clashes of light bulbs and lightning bugs, throngs of shadows and stones. Their bodies floated, pale as fallen doves, on the watery mirror of the summer night, God's pupil. God's blind eye. Now they were fish. No, sharks. They sunk their teeth into the lake as if it were a hunk of flesh. They were hungry, and it was nighttime, but the artificial light of a camera made them spin toward a twisted tree and glimpse Nella through the darkness, hidden under three branches shaped like open hands. She scuttled backward on her eight timid spider legs and looked them in the eyes for the first time.

There were shadows, not swans.

Something dangerous extended in the silence, something like cauldrons of bats across their foreheads.

And she ran.

Diego and Eduardo chased her into the forest. They were naked and hungry; they were also furious with the irritating spider who dodged branches, rocks, raised roots, clumsily leaping over the dry ground, plunging into the sepulcher of docile plants. They caught her in the middle of a clearing, laughing at her fear revealed among the foliage, and snatched her camera and surrounded her with their nakedness. She knew she was trapped by an all-encompassing sky, but she kept her eyes open. Diego pushed into her back and licked an ear while Eduardo put his hooked finger in her mouth. Nella shook: screams throbbed in her eyes, but she didn't dare let them out. The trees looked like the bars of a giant cage opening, but not for her. They were naked and hungry. Diego bit her neck as if it were a pillow, and she moaned. The sound of her fear lulled the birds in their nighttime nests. Eduardo allowed himself a smile before knocking her with a blow onto the leaves torn by the forest's breath. They dripped the forest. Diego lifted her up by the hair. This time Nella tried to get away, but they pinned her down. You better stop following us, gray fish, brown spider, they told her. She had the body of a twelve-year-old girl. Diego and Eduardo laughed when they caught her looking at their stiff penises with astonishment. We don't like you, they blurted out. Nella's eyes were owl tombs. Eduardo turned the camera on and played with the buttons until he found the photographs of a still animal chasing smaller, weaker ones. Suddenly, as if ash had started to fall, he forgot what he was doing. Diego let Nella go and moved closer to his friend, who was staring directly into the light of the camera, distracted. They dripped the forest. Nella seized her chance to leave slowly, with a strange calm that seemed genuine. Maybe she was never scared, they reflected hours later, fully dressed in their room.

Someone like that can't be afraid of us.

XI

Sometimes Eduardo read César Vallejo's poem "XIII" to Diego before bed:

> I think about your sex.
> My heart simplified, I think about your sex,
> before the ripe daughterloin of day.
> I touch the bud of joy, it is in season.
> And an ancient sentiment dies
> degenerated into brains.
>
> I think about your sex, furrow more prolific
> and harmonious than the belly of the Shadow
> though Death conceives and bears
> from God himself.
> Oh Conscience,
> I am thinking, yes, about the free beast
> who takes pleasure where he wants, where he can.
>
> Oh, scandal of the honey of twilights.
> Oh mute thunder.
>
> Rednuhtetum!
> (TR. CLAYTON ESHLEMAN)

XII

Nella's pictures almost always had dead animals in the foreground. Some had been photographed birthing organs like red fruits from their bellies; some appeared without eyes, without paws, without ears, without a tongue, dismembered, with melted expressions, like the incomplete images of a tangled, breathing puzzle. Diego and Eduardo found two photos of a gray rat, little and gutted, between her thirsty thighs; three in which a squirrel's body lay on top of her almost-flat naked chest with two little lilac hills they wanted to touch; four that showed the process of digging her big toe into a cat's yellow eye; and one in which her small ovular face, marked by pleasure, was covered in a thick layer of fresh blood.

Nella, they concluded, the spider, the fish, was a dark, obscene oasis amid shoes and ties and shirts and backpacks and chalkboards and numbers and letters. An oasis beyond the border. She was the fire of the hostile, the blow of the invincible. She was tundra, cyclops, Ferris wheel: what they were looking for to renovate and learn all the ways of falling.

They sighed. They smiled.

They'd found their Simone.

Interviewee: El Cuco Martínez

Location: Sor Rita Bar, Carrer de la Mercè, 27, 08002, Barcelona

"There's a myth going around that says the first porno movie in history was filmed in Argentina. They called it *El Sartorio* or *El Satario,* though who knows why if the thing was about a satyr. I don't know what the hell a sartorio or a satario is, do you? Anyway, they say jealous smutty-film collectors are hoarding the only copies of the tape. Yeah, you can picture those tíos in their enormous golden chalets, stacking cash on the table to buy works of art, fat tíos bored of getting everything they want . . . Assholes. Idiots who could end hunger in a third-world country if they felt like it. There are a lot of those types in the Deep Web, let me tell you, because there, if you want to, you can find illegal traffickers of art and more: you can find whoever you want, the possibilities are endless if you know how to work it, if you search carefully, and especially if you stay away from the hackers. The hackers are always scumbag sons of bitches, let me tell you. There are film stills circulating that supposedly come from the movie, but there's no way to know if they're real. No one even knows if *El Sartorio* was ever filmed or if it was totally made up and just got repeated so often that it seeped into reality, so those rumors about people getting a glimpse of it are impossible. What people do know, though I don't know how, is that it's about a satyr who spies on a group of nymphs playing by a lake, and when the poor devil gets horny, he decides to kidnap and rape one of the little sluts. It's a pretty rough story, yeah, but what's interesting is that the satyr is described as a hairy, horned monster, and you know what that means? That the movie, if it really exists, also introduced bestiality to porn cinema. I dunno, I dunno, I think it's funny that the experts talk about *Sartorio* and recount the plot as if they'd seen it with their own eyes, but no one has a copy, which means no one can actually say: Yes, I've seen it. You know what I think? Well, the same thing as the Teráns: that it doesn't matter if the movie exists or not, just like it doesn't matter that satyrs are mythological creatures or demons, that amateur porn videos aren't amateur, or that people having sex on camera aren't enjoying it even a little bit. It's enough that *El Sartorio* is believable; it's enough that the story awakens our pornographic imagination, that it doesn't need to be accurate, just plausible, like everything else in life, and sometimes not even that, just a light dose of possibility. What's possible isn't always plausible, but it has the force of a tsunami. Do you want another beer? It's on me. The siblings said, with good reason, that there are two ways to face our humanity: digging into the sky or digging into the earth. Clouds or worms. Sky-blue or black. Normally we all dig into the sky, because only crazy people look down and excavate. Supposedly we want the immensity, not our own but the one that's beyond us, that's always far away from skin and bones, far away from the dust to which we'll return and use to feed the grass. I'll tell you one thing, and this I learned with the Teráns, it's always better to dig into the earth. It isn't the easy path. It's painful, yes, but all knowledge is a splinter, embedded and impossible to remove. Looking up, climbing clouds, getting farther and farther away from yourself and what you are, you can come to know your painting, but never yourself. Because yeah, man, don't look at me like that: we're knowable, even if it's an unstable, broken knowing, we can explore ourselves like a cave. The siblings knew themselves. They knew their quicksand, and that in itself is a lot, tío. Fuck. What do you want me to say? The siblings were plausible and possible. That was enough for me."

Emilio Terán, age 17. Writer of rectangles.
Surfer of forums with deep holes.
Blue room with a bullet hole.

It gets dark. It's a lie that Dad loves us. I like empty space when I'm alone and still, but now I'm with my sisters, and I prefer them over solitude. Irene is painting her nails bubblegum pink and Cecilia is looking at the round fishbowl: she doesn't want to feed Gog. It's the second day of the fish's starvation in his water cage. We're in an air cage because it's a lie that Dad loves us. Sometimes Gog bangs his face against the glass. I don't know if fish are intelligent. I don't know if they know they're going to die. Irene moves her leg the wrong way, and the little jar of polish falls and stains her thighs like when Dad loves us less. She tucks her hair behind her Bambi ears and spreads the polish around with her fingers like when Dad orders her to be good. I don't think Mom loves us either. Irene laughs, and I laugh with her because I like her laughter, her face, her thighs. Cecilia doesn't know how to laugh, but it doesn't matter. Her hair is oily from yesterday, her skin sticky. Irene walks on tiptoe and smears the bubblegum-pink polish on her face. Her laugh explodes: she tickles me. Cecilia doesn't stop looking at Gog and doesn't care about being dirty. Dad calls her piggy, oinker, porker. His videos are called piggy.avi. Today I downloaded babyj.avi, tigger.avi, bathtime.avi, and bunnies.avi. I did my chores. Dad will be happy, which means he'll be nice to us. His nickname is xxBigBossxx. I look out the window: the yard gets dark, the pool moonshines, but that verb doesn't exist. Now it exists.

They told me I should start writing down everything I see. I'll write down everything I see because it's the only thing I am. The literature teacher doesn't know my name. She mixes me up with the guy next to me, and I don't like that. Irene would never forget my name. Cecilia would never forget who I am. The teacher doesn't know I'm different from the boy next to me and in front of me. If I told her what I see, she'd know the difference. I see a bullet hole in my bedroom wall. It's a deep tunnel like my father's anus. Once I tried to run away and they shot at me and hit the wall. The noise destroyed everything, but I came back. I see Irene moan and drool on the carpet. I see Cecilia's small breasts bouncing. I see the silence because it isn't invisible. Dad liked it better before, but we grew up. We grew up and Dad shot at us in many ways. I see my hands on the floor and my body at a strange angle. I hate seeing myself: I see myself. We grew up with our hearts buzzing. One day what I see will be like other things. My love for them, though, will not. Dad films us less. I see his bulging eyes and half-open mouth when he watches bathtime.avi. I see bathtime.avi. Irene laughs at the look on his face when he ejaculates. When we're alone, I kiss her and see we'll always be together. I see Cecilia's steps and all her darkness; I know I'll save her from her experience, I know we'll always be together. It won't be long until we can leave. Dad says he'll let us run away. We'll study in Guayas with all the insects. We grew up. Now I can force Mom to put her hands on the tundra of the ground. The world is that tundra where I put my hands. My name is teddy00.avi.

The ground is green, and we flop onto the flowers as if they were our beds. There aren't any clouds. The sun paints Irene's knees, and I remember her wounds. I wish there was always this much light refracting my mistakes. I wish everything would glow and come back to life. Kids are playing in the park. There's a woman with a weathered face selling lottery tickets who approaches the mothers and nannies. Cecilia takes her shoes off to rub her feet on the flowers. She squishes them and looks like she wants to laugh. I like hurting nature, she says. I think: It's so hard to hurt nature when the birds hide. There's so much to step on today, tomorrow, the day after. There are so many flowers, so many birds and trees, so much grass getting tangled in our teeth. Cecilia grabs my hand and asks me to lick her feet. I want to, but there's too much light and I get uncomfortable. Then the sky gets thick and gray. The children hug their mothers' legs. The forest breath makes our skin prickle. I see flies, and the ground glistens with ash. A volcano has vomited all its rage on us, Irene says, stretching out her flowery hand. The birds scream, "This is Quito. This is your home." I understand the alarm and close my eyes.

My mother never looked for us. We grew up in a house made of lichen where the silence spread from one end to the other and rocked us as if we could fall asleep with our mouths closed, but no: we opened our talking eyes. Irene and Cecilia always talked to me in cold sunrise languages. We'd walk to school bundled up in hard words and smiling at the sidewalks of the childhood path. I'd touch their hands and find my body shot so many times, but we didn't lose the childhood hanging from our necks; we didn't set our ears or legs free to run. The fragility of being six was a pile of rotten vegetation I used to make my bed. The fragility of being six didn't let me sleep or bury myself in the edges of a blue wall. My mother always watched us from a narrow corner. She knew what Dad was doing to us. She knew how to read our faces, and that's why she pinned up her hair. She never looked for us. Sometimes we watched Dad's documentaries in the theater. His name was followed by applause and newspaper reviews. Sometimes I was called the son of Fabricio Terán because they didn't know I was teddy00.avi. No one knew my name or the sound of my screams. Dad's documentaries about the Huaoranis and Taromenanes had little in common with teddy.vs.piggy.vs.bunny.avi. I always wanted to tell Mom that it was her job to look for us, but I don't know what a mother's duties are. I always wanted to tell her that I buried broken compasses under her pillow. Now I throw them away.

I see the only one: a pile of bodies that are mine. I see Aliciaxx, a pre-teen, in a hotel room. I see her swollen nipples. I see two men ejaculating into her coin-purse mouth. I see her make a face of disgust and smile as if it were the same thing; as if revulsion and happiness were so close in her heart. I see Babyj. She's a year or two old. I see her father fuck her in the ass while pressing her face into the carpet. I see Babyshi. She's three. I see her tied up and raped for the first time. I see her screams and her wail that's like a cascade of rocks shattering onto the ground. I see Babylexxxa. She's under a year old. Her father calls her a dirty bitch and pisses on her face like Dad did. I see Asianbunnie. She's fourteen. The_White_Whale fucks her in the ass and sticks two fingers in her vagina. She bleeds drops of purple love. She bleeds and stains the mountains of the landscape of bodies that drain. I see CatGodess. She's twelve. Her father pulls her hair while mounting her in a blue attic. I see Cbaby. She's three. I see her screams that say "IT HURTS, IT HURTS," big and bright like movie theater signs. I see Chiharu. She's eleven. I see her underground Lolita series. I see Daphne. She's nine. I see her mother hit and tie her to the bed so she can stick a dildo up her vagina. I see Ely. She's seven. Her father serves her his sperm in a wooden spoon. I see Jenny. She's ten. Her spiked necklace looks like a plant in the middle of the landscape of bodies that drain. I see TommyG. He's thirteen. I see his father order him to lick a dog's penis: I see him lick a dog's penis. I see Lada. She's seven. I see Elizabeth. She's fifteen. I see them helping their father rape their little sister, Mandy, who is red and crying in the bed of a black truck. I see Maryanne. She's five. She sticks her fist up her father's ass with her eyes closed. I see Pae. She's four. Her mother sticks her tongue in her vagina and her index finger in her anus. I see Veronika. She's twelve. I see her father and brother fuck her at the same time. I see landscapes of bodies that drain. I see everything that has been committed. I see Dad jacking off to the videos. I see tombs of laughter, plains of fears. Dust. Wind. I see my need to say that I watch landscapes of bodies that drain the color from all the nights. I see a pile of bodies that are mine: the only one. Teeth.

I touch Irene when Dad isn't there, and it's like it's the first time. She smiles. I love you, she says. Her face lights me up and all the volcanoes sleep. For the first time we aren't instruments. For the first time we want to. Her body is like mine: it drains, it unravels . . . I can see myself in all her holes, and that's love. Cecilia watches us from the doorway. I don't know if she stays quiet or cries. I don't know if she'd want Irene to touch her when Dad isn't there. She presses her toes into the ground and bends them. You prefer Irene, she tells me. I prefer hillsides, boats, rivers, houses. I prefer to belong and not be forced to be a puppet. There are moments like this when I'm mine, I tell her. She wrinkles her nose: She's so serious and opaque. I love her so much. Irene smiles and asks her to get naked. Cecilia sticks her tongue out but obeys. It's a lie that we're obedient: only when we're together, because we've decided to break into pieces. We catapult ourselves toward a landscape of bodies that drain. One day I'll bite the controlling hands, and I'll swallow all the ivy.

I see Irene. She's eight. I see Dad spreading her legs and running his tongue along her vagina. I see the red light of the camera blinking. I see Cecilia. She's six. I see her crawling naked and eating Dad's shit like a dog. I see her retches and dead doves. I see Dad's piss landing in my open mouth. The red light of the camera shines, and I see myself. I'm seven. Dad forces me to stick a finger in Irene, and she screams while we pretend we're Hollywood stars. I see the frozen floor deforming my hands: they're little and veiny. They're tools of torture. I see my pain when Dad sticks his enormous penis up my ass. My pain, I can say it, is wet, round, full, and steady. If I say how much it hurts, maybe dawn will break over the landscapes I see. But I'm tiny, and Dad walks on me because I'm tiny. I see my holes where Cecilia looks, and I know that's love. I know I embody the landscape of thousands of drained bodies. I know I can say it and it's my duty to say everything I can. That's why Irene says: Write everything you see. That's why Cecilia says: Write the only one. Sometimes I write many things I haven't seen until I put them on a sheet of paper. Then those things get dark. And it's like when the wall got a hole shot in it.

It's Mom's birthday. Irene makes her breakfast, and Cecilia watches Gog floating on the surface of the bubbly water. We have to throw him out, Dad tells her. But I want to keep the body, Cecilia says. A floating corpse is like a dream. Dad puts a present on the table and takes Mom by the hand. It looks like they love each other. Maybe they do love each other. The sun beats on the window, and the chocolate cake we bring to our mouths is bitter. We plan a picnic in the forest. We plan to have fun even though it's impossible. Irene and I exchange looks that irritate Mom. A floating corpse is like a dream. We comfort ourselves in absurdity, bitterness, and stupidity, but she doesn't like it. She'd rather we look at everything with a bullet hole in our foreheads, she'd rather we have statue eyes. Instead, we're alive, and we dream of bridges because in our house a floating corpse is like a dream. We discover that Dad's intelligence has crutches. He can't catch us. We run faster and faster with our eyes closed. Stupidity is evil, Irene says. She thinks we're free because we're intelligent, but only dead Gog is free. It'll be wonderful when we die, I say. Our bodies will go on without us and they'll shrivel up in the flowers. Cecilia widens her eyes and says that only a floating corpse is like a dream. Mom opens the present and cries. It isn't out of happiness.

Cecilia draws what she can't say. She draws her mouth always sealed with tongues that can't bend. She rides them by night. She rides them by day. I know what she's thinking because she's my sister and my mirror. I know that in her eyes the letters are empty figures like plump craters. Irene and I clear the fog by naming everything alive. Cecilia strips the verb conjugations we make and rides them. Your words are only shadows in the forest, she tells me, as her mouth spits geometries of deserts and volcanoes onto my temple. I try to make words have a meaning other than what they tell us. I try to make my own diction of the world. Cecilia kills off the meanings, though. Her silence is the flesh of my fear.

I see the only one: everything. I see this that is my blood and Irene's and Cecilia's spilling onto the tundra of the floor, my blood that's hot like my breathlessness, I see it steaming, spilling onto the cold, and spreading away from my shell. This is what it means to be naked, I think, and I see my nakedness lost in the blood I spill and that's

Irene's and Cecilia's because it's mine. I see poppy fields that are the puddles of my blood populating the earth. I see indestructible nature swallowing up my blood. We aren't sad: we're alive, and we aren't sad. My blood that spills flourishes in the earth and in the water and forces the paths of the landscapes of bodies that drain; I see them dawning dispossessed and covering what I see with everything I am. My raging blood courses through the mesetas, the volcanoes, it climbs up to the sky and floats like a corpse or like a dream. I see Irene and Cecilia spilling onto my heart shot into the wall of the sea, and I embrace them because they're the only one, and I say: Hello, tundra of my blood. Hello.

Interviewee: Iván Herrera

Location: Starbucks, Col. Hipódromo Condesa, 06100, Mexico City

"They stayed in touch with their parents and asked them for money, yes. That's why I never suspected they were making money off their piracy site. They didn't need it. Maybe they did it for fun, like *Nefando*, or because they wanted to start their own business."

"Maybe they didn't want to keep asking their parents for money."

"I don't think so. When we were roommates, they always accepted their parents' help with an ear-to-ear grin, a great big smile, güey, like a horseshoe. They had plenty of dough, so they lent us everything we needed when we needed it, especially El Cuco. I always thought their parents were well off, maybe diplomats or politicians, because how else could they keep supporting their kids so easily? Imagine my surprise when I found out what they'd done to them. No fucking way. I'll never understand how they were still talking to each other."

"You found out from *Nefando*."

"No. I heard it directly from one of the siblings."

"Oh really?"

"One night we curled up in the living room to watch a Swedish movie, I think, about the life of some guy who kidnapped kids to fuck them. We were sitting there, watching the movie and talking, because that's what we always did when we watched something together, we had that in common: the uncontrollable impulse to talk about what we were watching. We were relaxed, or better put, they were relaxed, because the movie made my hair stand on end. I don't remember her exact words, but out of nowhere Irene said her father had done the same thing to them. I took it as an awkward joke at first, not because it seemed impossible, but because she said it smiling and looking for the Telepizza number in the phone book. But Cecilia and Emilio didn't bat an eye; they kept drinking and talking about the shots in the movie, even though they'd definitely heard their sister's abrupt confession. I laughed, though I didn't find it funny at all, and I told Irene something like you don't joke about that kind of thing, you know, the bullshit you say when this kind of thing comes up, and Cecilia looked me up and down and said she could prove it because their father had put videos on the internet. I still wasn't having it, but I started to feel bad because the joke was awkward and the light mood had gotten heavy, frankly. After ordering a pepperoni pizza with extra cheese, Irene told me, as if it were no big deal, that she was going to prove they weren't lying, and she got this competitive look on her face, you know? As if we both thought we were right and were going to see who'd win. I don't think I could begin to tell you how disoriented and uncomfortable I felt . . . I even thought I was going to throw up. When she turned on her laptop, I wanted to tell them to fuck off, but I chickened out. I was afraid they'd tease me, that they were messing with me just to see how I'd react. I remember Emilio paused the movie, as if it were obvious we'd keep watching, and Cecilia sat down next to me with a María Félix attitude I'd never seen before, very feminine and haughty. Irene pressed play on the video and . . . I don't know what else to tell you. I've seen a lot in my life, but not three people ready to enthusiastically show footage of their own rapes. I remember feeling that they were crazy and sick, very sick, but now I think they learned to deal with the past in a peculiar way and didn't see themselves as victims."

"The siblings told you that?"

"No, but I'm convinced it's true. In my opinion, there are two fundamental responses to this kind of situation: the first is to assume the role of the victim, which means you're the kind of person who narrates your life as resulting from a chain of uncontrollable, unfortunate events in which others have taken advantage of you or somehow fucked you over. The second is to assume the role of the perpetrator, that is, the person responsible for fucking everyone else over. It seems to me they chose the second role. They didn't feel sorry for themselves.

None of the three were pitiful like that. They talked about their ass-hole of a father the same way I'd talk about mine. To tell you the truth, I don't think they thought what their father did to them was all that bad. I mean, it didn't seem like the end of the world to them. They also weren't ashamed to tell anyone who wanted to know or was prepared to listen. That doesn't mean they told just anyone, but they told me, and I was never their friend, we just lived together. Maybe they accepted their past because in the end it brought them good things. Their relationship, for example."

"Yes, I already know about that."

"They didn't hate their parents either. They looked down on them and used them, but they didn't hate them. Or maybe they were very good at hiding their hatred and living beyond it, which is good."

"You don't think *Nefando* was a way of expressing their hatred?"

"Why do you say that? *Nefando* was a work of redefined love, not hatred."

"What do you mean?"

"It was a space for personal exploration. You could think differently while playing. The Teráns designed it so that the player's experience was a poem."

"Not everyone shares that opinion, let me tell you."

"Poems aren't pleasant, at least the good ones. Any poetry worth its salt will let you fall. It's impossible not to be broken after that."

Kiki Ortega, age 23. FONCA scholar.

Room #1

It's so hard, she thought: I don't want my words to be a block, or a city, or a factory; I want them to be like the grass. Can they be like the grass? She sat down at an empty, round, tooth-white table and turned on her laptop. The shelves around her formed a square with open corners, and she thought this was the perfect state to write: trapped in broken geometry. *I don't want to build anything; I'm not interested in being a language engineer: I'm only looking to nurture what's already living.* Some twenty meters away the librarian was chewing a piece of gum as if ruminating on her own foul temper; occasionally, every five minutes or so, she blew her nose and threw the Kleenex into a pink bin. The watery sound of her snot didn't seem to disturb the elderly gentlemen occupying the other tables in the room, their faces hovering over the history books, their lips dried out by the heat, their eyes disappearing from their wrinkly faces, men whose very presence made the library feel like the inside of a nursing home. *They're so hard, grammatically correct sentences. I wonder if I'll be brave enough to write poorly.* Aging was a mystery with deep roots that didn't interest her much, at least for now. To novelize Nella, Diego, and Eduardo, she'd have to return to the most dangerous period of life: childhood. She, who'd survived it, feared it like an infected needle dancing above her cornea, but she accepted the sensation because writing with fear is far better than writing with indifference. *Being blinded by memories of the early years is easy but wrong.* Perhaps the elderly, survivors of their own childhoods, wanted to return to their earliest fragility because they were experiencing the later one with an insurmountable boredom. Nevertheless, for her there was no hell scarier than the one you cross barefoot as a child. *I wonder if I'll be brave enough to write blind.* She'd survived her childhood with her fingers cut and tongue tied; she'd overcome that phase of horrors by desperately wanting to grow up. *Adulthood is the loss of the fragile.* Now she had to remember it: she had to confront writing like that continual stuttering, like that excess, or else not write at all. *Because writing is like childhood.* She relaxed her muscles and fearfully returned to the memory of when she showed her first story to her mother; she read it from a hammock, clenching her jaw and flaring her nostrils. "Don't ever write this crap again," she said, ripping up the paper and taking the shreds away forever. But Kiki kept writing the same crap in which she unknowingly eroticized house pets and other animals that lived in the schoolyard, and she also wrote the bad words a girl should never utter but which everyone said on the street and on TV and even in school, lowering their voices, cupping their hands into a shell around their mouths or immediately swallowing the words as soon as they were out. *Nella, Diego, and Eduardo are the childhood-like writing.* Back then she stuttered in an attempt to look at the world for the first time. That's why she kept writing: because she couldn't draw houses, families, or trees, but she could recount the images of life in her own way. *Irreverence is like the writing that drinks from the well of setbacks.* Her second story was kidnapped by her literature teacher, a woman with an acne-ridden face, who turned the story in to the principal, who called her mother, who hit her with a shoe and a science book and then sat her down at a square table with the second story open—the narrative at the heart of the dispute—and explained, or at least tried to, that what she was doing was bad, that her story was pornographic and pornography was dirty and contemptible, and it made others believe she was a dirty and contemptible girl, and this was bad, really bad, because girls should only write nice things, white as a tablecloth or a page in a notebook, things like clouds, smiles, and butterflies. "But this is beautiful to me," she said, still crying over her second story. And her mother shook her head as if there were a vase teetering on her shoulders to tell her she'd have to punish her, although it pained her to the core, until she understood the difference between

beautiful and horrible. *Stumbling is essential for narrating the fallen.*
She dragged her to an empty trunk set against the wall and locked
her inside. *Where would she find the courage to write poorly?* The light
went out in that wooden prison. In front of her, a few meters away in
the library, an old man watched quietly, perched like a church gar-
goyle. The darkness inside the trunk had a coarse texture and smelled
of a mildew she associated with the word "childhood." She crouched
in that box for hours and screamed and yelled because her body hurt,
her fear hurt, but her mother didn't let her out until it was night and
the trunk had become the world. *Nella, Diego, and Eduardo are characters who run the risk of falling apart, and she wants them to have a
certain substance.* There were stories that made her curl up for so
long that she had no choice but to piss herself. The first time was the
worst, but then she got used to the warmth of her own fluids. *I was
tortured because of a story, she thought, I was tortured for years and
never learned to say: I won't write again.* She soon learned that growing up meant her bones wouldn't fit in a trunk someday, but also that
there would be bigger, dustier imprisonments, captivities so inescap-
able they'd strip meaning from any attempt to get away. *The difference between the beautiful and horrible is the same as the difference
between the inside and outside of the trunk: there is none.* The gargoyle-
old-man didn't take his eyes off her, and she started to enjoy it.
Everyone else's old age made her feel young, breathe deeply, and swell
with all the hours she'd spent curled up because of her stuttering
writing. *The gaze of the gargoyle-old-man was the simulacrum of any
marsupial's, a zephyr making her belly flutter, a door that led her into
the tranquility of her enormous confinement—the privilege of adulthood.* The only inherent problem of her age was that no word was
prohibited, no discourse, no narration too scandalous, too subver-
sive, too rampant. That force had vanished with childhood. Now, to
recount her torture by writing a story, to learn to pronounce what
had been taken from her, she had to swim far from her navel and not
drown in her own waters. *It is difficult to pull away from yourself. No:
it is impossible.* She felt the gaze of the gargoyle-old-man trespassing
the blank page of the Word document like an invitation. *She wouldn't*

write: she'd shove the grant up her ass, and she wouldn't write. She was exhausted by searching for the body in its animal aspect. *Only moans were more important than silence: moans strong as her breath.* She spread her legs and brought her hand toward her narrative core. The gargoyle-old-man slid his eyes down, and she was sure that despite the position of the tables and the distance, he could tell what she was doing with her body amid so much silence. *Nella, Diego, and Eduardo might turn out to be unrealistic, but realism is a ghost holding up its own skull.* The circles on her clitoris started melting slowly into spirals of heat. *You have to read and write accepting the holes.* She tucked her underwear to one side and slipped in two fingers, slow as a sinking ship, never breaking eye contact with her lover, the gargoyle-old-man: all her muscles tensed up in that gaze that was once a bonfire and now a leaden wasteland. *I need a writing that moans through irony to say that I survived my childhood.* Her fingers got wet, and her chest sunk. The gargoyle-old-man didn't care that she was looking at him while she masturbated, and that was the sweetest thing about the shared pleasure. *One day I'll recount my childhood so well that I'll fill the blank sheets and slither toward my other ages.* The first time she touched herself she was eight years old and locked in the trunk, breathing erratically, thinking she'd die from her fifth story: a story about the circus affair between a red-headed dwarf and an elephant. Never, in any of the punishments imposed by her mother, had she experienced such a strong attack of claustrophobia as she did that day. *A writing that is like grass or a flowerpot wouldn't be so bad, she thought.* On TV she'd seen the ostentatious elephant penises, so she imagined the overflowing love of a circus dwarf for a creature whose sex could go all the way through her. *The eyes of the gargoyle-old-man didn't go through her: they only gently penetrated her.* In the trunk, suffocating, bathed in sweat, she remembered the scene in her story in which she recounted the dwarf's decision to die for love; she reminisced on the glorious moment when the elephant impaled her with his enormous, curved phallus and how the pain and pleasure peaked with death. *She couldn't write any other literature that wasn't made of her reduced I: the I that wanted to learn to think.* Then she felt something like desire surging from her deepest anguish, a trembling that briefly paralyzed her and later mobilized her and made her caress her vulva, wet from the pee she didn't know how to hold. *I want to write so I can do justice to my shame.* She masturbated while suffocating inside a trunk, rabidly feeling her impulses, because she thought she was going to die, just as she now masturbated in her wordless shame.

And she suddenly decided: *My shame will be the bastion of my novelized tongue.*

She stopped touching herself and placed her fingers on the keyboard.

Community gamers forums. Deep Web.
Summary of posts and accounts about *Nefando,*
browser game. Original language: English.
Translation (and suspected rewriting) by Kiki Ortega.

[TOPIC: *Nefando* change of address]
April 10 at 7:00 p.m.
Cyborges*
They moved the site again. Here's the new link:
nefjkando78gum6z.onion
   Enjoy!

[TOPIC: *Nefando* . . . how do you play?]
April 12 at 2:00 p.m.
KiLLPRO*
Started playing last night, still don't get it. There are no
instructions. No demo either. Can someone help?
Doctor_Roxo*
HAHAHAHAHAHAHA

[TOPIC: *Nefando* link]
April 20 at 10:00 p.m.
CirioPeeledPlums*
Does anyone have it?
Bersek98*
No

[TOPIC: *Nefando,* the experience]

May 17 at 8:00 p.m.

<u>ClockWorkxX*</u>

Some of us were lucky enough to play *Nefando* before it disappeared from the web. I feel privileged, and I suspect all of us who witnessed this moment of gaming HISTORY will remember our unique, private odyssey FOREVER . . .

I have yet to read two accounts that are exactly alike, but that doesn't mean there are infinite storylines. The first step to completing the puzzle is to write what we saw. *Nefando,* or the journey into the bowels of a room, can be understood as a book with multiple readings in which each player, spectator, or [insert the noun that best describes your participation in the adventure here] makes it their own.

This is my account of the game: klomHjsAMzxwLqtr.onion I'd love to read yours.

Let's share our experiences, my fellow chosen ones!

[GAME ACCOUNTS:
SELECTION OF FRAGMENTS FROM THE USERS
WE'LL CALL—BECAUSE WHY NOT—A, B, AND C]

[A]

General observations: For now, there's a blue room and a woman sleeping. She's naked, lying face up on a white mattress that engulfs her black hair, her dark skin, and her chest, which rises and falls. There are no windows. It's an ordinary room, though too neat and empty. It doesn't look lived in, not even by her, the unmoving woman. There's one door, a closet, and a desk with a computer and notebook. The first thing I did was move the cursor over the objects. Nothing. Then I clicked on the sleeping woman as if I were smacking her awake. I hit her several times in the face, chest, and belly. She didn't wake up. She was breathing. Her body moved slightly with each blow. Now her arm is dangling off one side of the bed. I don't know what it means. As expected, clicking on the door, the closet, the computer, the notebook didn't take me anywhere. The room fills the whole screen: it's a fixed viewpoint, and the light is dim. It looks like I can't leave. I stop hitting the woman and wait.

[B]

After trying everything in the room and hitting the sleeping woman until I got bored (her boobs are magnificent, I punched them so many times they're black and blue and there will be blood if I keep going, I think I could click her to death and she'd never wake up, maybe I should kill her just to see what happens, maybe that's what you're supposed to do), I clicked the light bulb hanging from the ceiling and it shattered. The room went black, but I could still make out the outlines of the objects inside. I waited a few minutes, maybe five, maybe eight. Nothing happened, so I started again.

[C]

All I can hear is her steady breathing. I think she's been drugged and kidnapped. I bet no one else has thought of that.

[A]

Every game demands certain virtues of its players: the first on *Nefando*'s list is patience. Being patient, i.e., waiting as long as it takes, is what gets real results in this game. The first virtue is an endurance test, but the second is even more complicated because it involves an intensive observation process. In *Nefando*, it seems like there's nothing to look at, but the simplicity of the room is misleading. The question you have to ask is: What am I not seeing? What is hiding in the crevices of the everyday, right there in plain sight?

[B]

Nothing changed, so I broke the light bulb again to look at the outlines. It was like before, so it occurred to me to click on the dark outlines. The computer turned on.

[C]

It's four forty-five in the morning, and I made an exciting discovery: next to her bed, barely visible, there's a switch that lets me turn off the light. It isn't total darkness, though. It seems like I'm the only window where a little light gets in. The important thing is that the closet door opens when there's no light. It seems empty inside, but I can't be sure. If I click on the switch, the closet door closes again.

[A]

There's so much waiting and watching that it looks like the sleeping woman's pubic hair is growing.

[B]

The computer has been on for over two hours, but I can't log on because it's asking for a password. I tried: "blue," "room," "bed," "naked woman," "sleeping woman," "sleeping," "nefando," but nothing works.

[C]

I read on a forum that you can drag the computer to the other side of the desk. I did and . . . Surprise! The machine was covering a hole in the wall.

[A]

I accidentally discovered that I could move the computer on the desk. Doing so revealed a little hole in the wall. It looks like a gunshot, but I can't get close enough to see. I can't click on it either. I'm getting impatient and kinda lost.

[B]

I hit the sleeping woman again because it was the only thing I could do. She finally started to bleed and stain the bed, barely lit by the glowing computer. I kept hitting her anyway until one of her legs dropped to one side, and on her calf you could read "Carmilla." I used this name to log on to the computer.

[C]

I turned off the light and the hole in the wall glowed as if there were a sun behind it. A video immediately popped up on the screen and showed a woman disemboweling a tethered dog with her stiletto. "MY CHILDHOOD: THIS DOG" was written across the image. All I could do was watch. Nothing was possible. I stopped playing for a few hours, but I didn't close the window. When I came back, the notebook on the desk was open.

[A]

I still don't understand the function of the hole in the wall, but tonight I discovered that if I leave the cursor over the sleeping woman's pubic hair, it grows profusely and falls to the side of the bed like a plant.

[B]

According to Wikipedia, *Carmilla* is the name of a novella by Joseph Sheridan Le Fanu about vampires. If the sleeping woman is Carmilla, maybe she's a vampire. That would explain the lack of windows and her unconscious state. Maybe it's daytime outside. Maybe *Nefando* is that kind of game.

[C]

There was an erotic story titled "Rebeca and the Black Panther" in the notebook, followed by these fragments:

1. "I went hunting a week ago and managed to shoot a deer. He was still alive when I approached, but then he died in my arms. It was delicious and arousing to watch his death throes. I stuck my finger in the warm hole the bullet left and came right there. I dream about that warmth every day and wake up drenched in love."
2. "Look at my pretty dog. I've had her tied up since yesterday: with a pair of socks stuffed in her mouth and my wife's dildo up her ass. At first she didn't like that I'd tamed her, because she's a wild animal, but then she realized who's in charge and now she has no choice but to accept how hard I'm going to fuck her up the ass."
3. "I tripped over a cat and brought him home tonight. He hasn't died yet. He barely breathes and seems to be suffering a lot. I ejaculated on him five times."

[A]

Something mysterious happened: the pubic hair bore into the floor and seems to be slowly pushing the sleeping woman off the bed. I decided not to move the mouse. Today I'm watching.

[B]

On the computer I could only access a folder containing more than a dozen .avi files with names like Teddy, Butterfly, and Piggy. I opened all of them. They're child pornography videos that the following phrases scroll across: "THIS IS HOW THEY RUIN YOU-THEY MAKE YOU A-SEWAGE-SYSTEM-BUT THE DAY-COMES AND YOU CAN SAY-I DO NOT FORGIVE YOU-AND PISS ON THE FORGIVENESS RITUAL-AND WALK DOWN A NARROW STREET ILLUMINATED BY ALL THE FILTH YOU CARRY WITHIN-WITHOUT SMILING-WITHOUT CRYING-DOWN THE STREET OF THE NAKEDDYING."

[C]

This afternoon the closet door opened all by itself and from its depths emerged a crocodile that's now wandering around the room. The letters on its scales read: "THIS ANIMAL: MY VOICE."

[A]

The pubic hair has also started growing upward and poking through the ceiling. The sleeping woman is still on the bed, but she's lying in a strange position, almost floating over the white sheet.

[B]

Yesterday I realized the sleeping woman changed after the blows. Her breasts got smaller and her hips less prominent. She looks like a teenager. I decided the only thing I could do was hit her again. I don't know how long I did it, but the blood rained down and it was good. I liked it a lot. The beating made the sleeping woman's body start to look like a child's. What was left on the bed was the bruised body of a little girl. She was still breathing when I stopped.

[C]

After five hours of prowling the room, the crocodile climbed onto the bed and started eating the sleeping woman. I realized I could hit it to make it stop, but I didn't. Now the animal rests, sated, on the red sheet.

[A]

I've opted for inaction because this, I now know, is not a game. I'm an observer of the phenomena presented to me. Many things have changed over the past forty-eight hours: the sleeping woman is suspended in midair, her pubic hair is growing toward the earth and toward the sky, and the hole in the wall has started spurting water. The room is slowly flooding. I sometimes see images amid the silence.

[B]

The sleeping woman was no longer there when I woke up.

[C]

An hour has passed since I closed the game forever. I clicked on the crocodile and heard a woman's screams. I'm not cut out for this kind of thing. I can't take it anymore. Good luck to everyone. Good-bye.

[A]

The room flooded four hours ago. The objects are floating. The notebook has opened and I can read four questions: "Do you want her hair?" "Do you want her fingernails?" "Do you want her skin?" "Do you want her sex?" This time, I don't know why, I click on the last question. Projected on the sleeping woman's body, on the bed, and on the walls, is a video of a man cutting off his penis. I force myself to watch. I have to watch everything. That's my role here. It's my sole responsibility.

[TOPIC: Is *Nefando* a horror game?]

May 5 at 12:00 a.m.

DivineFallacy*

I almost pissed myself when the sleeping woman disappeared from the room in the blink of an eye. The door's closed, but she could be in the closet, couldn't she? Or under the bed. Can anyone see what's under the bed?

Cartoon_Head*

My sleeping woman didn't disappear, but now she's sitting up on the bed. I can't hear her breathing anymore. This is starting to scare me.

[TOPIC: Carmilla isn't the password]

April 28 at 4:10 p.m.

Dren_Utogi*

For those of you playing *Nefando:* I wrote "Carmilla" and didn't get a positive result. I still can't log on.

Lunatich*

My sleeping woman doesn't have any tattoos.

Mibeshu*

My sleeping woman's tattoo says "Wanda."

[TOPIC: The videos in *Nefando*]

May 10 at 6:45 p.m.

Belimawr*

Some of the videos of animal torture that appear in the game have been circulating online for years. I found them on a necrozoophilia forum.

Will the same thing happen with the videos of the kids?

Interviewee: El Cuco Martínez

Location: Sor Rita Bar, Carrer de la Mercè, 27, 08002, Barcelona

"The police were investigating me because of the videos, yes, but when they corroborated my account and verified that the videos had been circulating online for years, they left me alone, the jackasses. In short, I didn't do anything, dammit. Even if they'd caught the Teráns before they left the country, what could they have done to them? Locked them up for using videos of their father raping them? They were the victims and that was their footage. The siblings had the right to do what they wanted with them, and that's what they did."

"And what did they do, according to you?"

"Fuck, I don't know. They said that forgiveness is an aporia, just like restorative justice; that some things can't be repaired, but that isn't necessarily bad. I don't know . . . When trust is broken, there's still a world afterward, it's just a world where rules don't matter. That's the world they lived in."

"Do you think they wanted to report their father?"

"No, they weren't interested in punishing him. They used him. They asked him for money, and that monster gave it to them with no objection whatsoever because he knew perfectly well what he'd done to them, and he knew that they could put him in jail if they wanted to."

"I don't get it."

"Of course not. In any case, it's their prerogative as victims to do what's best for them."

"So they forgave him. They forgave their father."

"No, tío, you don't understand anything. I already told you: they saw forgiveness and justice as an aporia, that's why they lived outside that realm and dealt with what had happened to them a different way."

"How?"

"I dunno, I dunno. I don't even know what I'm saying, tío, don't pay any attention to me."

Iván Herrera, age 25. Master in literary creation.

Room #2

It was midnight, and you went out for a walk in a park with paths broken like your flesh, Quetzalcoatl, paths licked by the hot wind of the sky closing in. Like yesterday, like tomorrow, you ate the hunger of ripe, turgid fears withdrawn under your tongue made rough by so many soliloquies without doors, without circles, without bent syllables recalling tunnels sown in your ear. You rabidly penetrated the mouth of the origins: a boulevard darkened by dusk but soon lit by the dawn expanding into the hidden corners of the park. You breathed in the calm, the ochre silence, the depths of the urbanized nature that often lulled you to sleep, Tezcatlipoca, but you didn't want to howl in nightmares that weren't yours. Above, the sky brushed against your head like a mother's hand and said "I forgive you" while the loathsome-you crouched in the rocky terrain of your body. Sometimes you needed to expel yourself, run away from yourself, take refuge in dark, open spaces, move so you could do something with the energy and with the hatred so pure it blinded you to tears. At night the park was a home of iron tombstones, the only possible shelter for your growing, disfiguring rage. You wondered what the epitaph would be for your serpent Quetzalcoatl, burly and future lifeless beast—maybe: "Here lies / the darkness: / the black sphere," or "Seduced by bad pleasures / I will return / to / bury myself"—as if the ceremony of your dead sex were something you'd been waiting for your whole life. You walked down broken paths, Tezcatlipoca, and on a distant bench, despite the bushes and the dark streetlamps, you thought you saw a couple fucking in the shadows. The trees swayed over them, gloomy, raining down their withered leaves, and you watched, hidden in the nocturnality of a prudent distance. She jumped on top, straddling him with her skirt hiked up around her waist, revealing flaccid glutes that made a clumsy slapping sound on impact. You were overcome with disgust and pain from your wrong body. You wore a mask of yourself, a crypt you had to damage before you could break away from your false *I*. You knew, plumed serpent, that you'd never enjoy sex, because the only thing you desired was to carefully destroy yourself, to peel off from the outside and the inside until you hit the rocky places burying you: memory. You were looking for some thorny memory, something to explain the loathsome-you, something like your father raping you, like what happened to the Teráns, or your mother sucking your dick, or a teacher forcing you to suck his, but none of that had happened to you, a city boy from Polanco. To justify yourself, you started inventing a past that wasn't yours, one full of traumas and little tortures, childhood stories that always aroused you and made it possible for you to rightfully assault your serpent Quetzalcoatl. You always wanted to make things hurt you. You always wanted to see how far you could go. You once tried to explain to Kiki that in order to write, you have to go beyond yourself: do what you wouldn't do, be what you aren't; in other words, throw yourself into feeling something beyond your limited emotional field, but she didn't understand what you were trying to tell her. "To write you have to be yourself, because that's all we can be," she said, not realizing she was hurting you. And you, smoking black mirror, shattered into a million knife-shaped pieces—you were used to breaking into shards. Kiki quietly told you it was important to look at everyone else while carefully looking at yourself. That's why she thought there wasn't anything behind your unpracticed queerness, your consensual virginity, and believed you were what you revealed: a pale lagoon where animals look at their timid reflections before they lower their heads to drink. You tried to tell her about your rockslide several times, the part you didn't share with anyone, but you stopped short, fearing scorn. "Güey, cut the bullshit and go get some already. Go fuck someone like you're gonna die tomorrow. Go fuck someone and to hell with your rich family and Mexican society that blesses their own butts every morning," she once told you, because she didn't understand your desire in the wrong—always nauseating—body; because she didn't know that what you were doing was washing yourself and slowly, with repugnance, with hysteria, ripping you out of yourself. That's how everyone unwittingly ignored you, though the same could be said by those you saw as transparent and one-dimensional. The same could be said by the smoking black mirror of the sky that was falling ever closer to you, or your own split soul that you'd resigned yourself to not understanding. You kept walking, as if this gait could grant you a less confusing face. Kiki was incapable of being someone else, but you, Tezcatlipoca, were two. You could also awaken more interlocutors in yourself. One afternoon after school, at least ten years ago, at the house of your then girlfriend Nabila, you imagined what it would be like to rape her right there, in the living room where you were watching television while her parents were at work. You didn't want to do it, you didn't want to have sex with her or make her suffer, but a savage curiosity suddenly throbbed, and you couldn't help but open yourself up to new possibilities. You wanted to know what you would be like if you were someone you weren't. And that crucial question made your head spin out of control. You tried to detach from your affection and managed to see Nabila as a lab rat. You were surprised by how easy it was to stop loving her. In a matter of seconds, because you thought about her differently, she was no longer a person. Nabila had her black hair pulled back into a high ponytail and was wearing a short skirt. You imagined what you'd feel if you hit her in the face and ripped off her uniform, if you acted like you were going to rape her, even though you knew you wouldn't be able to do such a thing, because your penis would never get hard. What was it that aroused rapists? you wondered. The feeling of power they got from subjugating another person, humiliating them, maybe, and that was something you couldn't feel, smoking black mirror, plumed serpent; you could only experience the desire to know what that felt like. And there was a throbbing curiosity in every corner of your body, altering you, giving you perhaps an even more atrocious name. You imagined the truth that you hated Nabila, that you were jealous of her nubile breasts, her young voice, her mamey-colored vulva, and you got up off the couch and climbed on top of her like the animal you now were. She looked startled, then irritated. You fixed your eyes on hers, wanting to show her you were no longer you and wanted to hurt her. You did everything you could to inscribe the nature of your thoughts in your eyes, like a message in a bottle, and you thought you'd succeeded when Nabila's face transformed in fear. She pushed you with her dry branch hands, refusing the shame of the intimidation, but she couldn't move you an inch, and you smiled, satisfied, feeling your heart beat like a constrictor machine within you. Then you brought your fingers under Nabila's skirt, and she tried to hit you with her fists and triangular knees, to really hit you, because now she was afraid of you, because now, somehow, she'd seen what you'd wanted her to see in your eyes, something instinctive and dangerous. You were so submerged in the role you were playing that you slapped her twice and stuck a finger into her vagina. Nabila screamed, started to cry, covered her face with her hands, and you didn't feel anything: not pleasure, hatred, or pity. Suddenly you were a wasteland. The emptiness froze your molars and calmed the loathsome-you. But you, serpent Quetzalcoatl, didn't want the cold to domesticate you. That's why you insisted on attacking her, and when she bit you, you hit her in the belly with such force that you saw her face go red and her chest sink in, distorted, stripped of air. The veins bulged in her neck like beautiful streams under her muddy skin. It was an instant that expanded inside you and felt sublimely beautiful: you were capable of hitting her just like an inanimate object without breaking down, without closing your eyes. You knew then that you could hurt others for the sake of nothing more than anthropological curiosity, that the cruelty burrowing into you was deeper than you thought, that you hated with great ease, and that the hatred was just the brief or prolonged desire for pain. That impulse was always mobilized by an internal violence that couldn't be trained, that had no reason for being other than to reveal itself. It was a centrifugal force shooting out like a rocket. In you, plumed serpent, smoking black mirror, you discovered a rage that no longer fit in its lair. And all thanks to Nabila, who never told anyone what you did to her, perhaps out of shame or because she loved you. The reason for her silence didn't really matter anymore, but that was what made you accept your need to expel yourself; that and the silence and that afternoon when you saw yourself as you were: a multiple monster, emptied of identity. And that was how you walked toward a tree to sit on one of its exposed roots. You were there, that night, with the darkness of the sky falling down on you, to escape from the loathsome-you that said it was time to cut off your wrong member. The idea had been gnawing at you for years, invading your dreams and unfeasible fantasies, but you'd known how to stop yourself when you punished your serpent Quetzalcoatl. The punishment soothed a more terrible yearning that drove you slowly. Your desire for pain, which you'd directed especially at yourself, never dominated you, never clouded your thoughts or disrupted your ever-deliberate trigger, but now you feared that your hands would tremble, Tezcatlipoca, and the rage would overcome you. You were unintentionally watching another unthinkable being emerge from you; unnamable, unpredictable, a cavity where insects and dirty waves seeped forth. Your bedroom dangerously enclosed you with the one who was still a stranger: that was why you'd fled to the park in the middle of the night and from the breath of the sky closing in, though the feeling of safety in the open air drained from your body with every passing. A four-legged shadow, panting, emerged from the bushes and trotted toward your shadow with its tongue out. You weren't afraid. You saw the little animal stop in front of you, eagerly wagging its tail. You didn't know it, and it didn't know you. You looked at it like a metaphor. You concluded it had gotten lost and its owner was surely looking for it somewhere. It was fat and well cared for. It was one of those expensive breeds you couldn't pronounce. The innocence of well-loved creatures encircled its snout. Its eyes fixed on yours with the docility of dawn. You thought, still sitting by the tree, that this experience was that moment when you fled from Nabila as she writhed in pain, and you knew: I'll only have the memory of this from now on. The construction of a personal memory let you appropriate experiences that weren't yours; to carry on after the banishment of you. The dog looked at you but couldn't read you; it didn't see in your eyes the loathsome-you emerging from the curiosity, from the desperation of a life without narrative, without self-awareness. The dog ignored the desire for pain that cast a shadow on your hands, and that's why it didn't run away from you, Tezcatlipoca. You wanted it to sense the danger, but when you reached out your hand to grab it by the scruff, it didn't resist. And then you wanted nothing but to reach the ultimate consequences of destruction: your power. The mystical experience was the experience of nothing, or rather, the experience of oneself. You were living through yourself. What else could you do? The dog's neck was so small that you only needed one hand to lift it up in the air and smash it into the trunk. Your body shuddered from something too big and abstract: something that came from the being you couldn't name. You slammed it against the tree with the full force of your hunger. Once: the shuddering howl of pain. Twice: an attempted grunt. Three times: the blood soaking you with warmth. Four times: the sound of breaking bones. Five times: the silence. Six times: and the silence. Seven times: and the silence. Eight times: and the silence. Nine times: and the silence. And the hush rising up from the rocky ground. And the silence repeated ten times. The memory died as you dropped the dog to the ground and got up, dizzy, but when you walked the broken paths, stained with death, the tree was still behind you, and so was the dog.

Interviewee: Kiki Ortega

Location: El Gato del Raval, Rambla del Raval, 08001, Barcelona

"The siblings were the first to leave. Iván and I found out they were going back to Ecuador on the day of their flight. We found them packing their bags one morning, and they just announced 'We're leaving,' as if it were no big deal. I think El Cuco already knew because he took the news in stride. I thought it was all a little abrupt. They just disappeared."

"And they didn't tell you what they were planning to do when they went back to their country?"

"No. Why would they have told me?"

"I don't know."

"I asked them once why they didn't go to class, why they were wasting their scholarship, and they said there was a lot to look at in the world before speaking. They said that—I can't remember which of the three—plus a line from a Gelman poem that goes 'the golden boars are eating Yvonne.' And I swear I didn't know it was a Gelman line, so you can imagine my reaction when they dropped it on me. That same day, without any apparent motive, they lent me his poetry collection *De palabra,* and days later, when I finally read it, I found the fucking line at the end of a poem about madness. The funny thing about this story, güey, is that 'the golden boars are eating Yvonne' had the same function in the poem as in my conversation with the Teráns. It wasn't a metaphor, but pure speech without referent, signifier without signified. That's when I thought I understood."

"What?

"That the golden boars are eating Yvonne."

"Oh."

"A month later the police showed up to ask us all sorts of questions. And we answered, of course. Just like you, they wanted us to describe the game in detail. Though they were really interested in Proyecto Cratos, not *Nefando*. All the same, they ended up taking it off the internet, you know, because of the child porn content."

"Did you watch the child pornography videos?"

"No. When I played, I saw a few videos of people cutting themselves and self-mutilating, but they were of legal age. I also saw images of mystic saints. I took the sleeping woman as someone experiencing a prolonged moment of ecstasy."

"So you had an ascetic reading of the game."

"Then I learned about the existence of Proyecto Cratos and that the siblings had sold it for a really good price. That's why I thought the police's supposed preoccupation with *Nefando* was hypocritical. I'm not even sure that's what they were actually investigating. I know, because El Cuco told me, that all the videos used in the game had been downloaded from the internet, which meant they'd been circulating for years on forums for pedophiles and other sickos, but apparently now it's a crime to use the world's smut, dredge it up from the sewers, and resignify it. I don't get it, güey. The Teráns didn't film those videos. They didn't rape or hurt anyone. I told the people who interrogated me, 'What? Now you're going to criminalize the victims?' And those assholes didn't say anything. I know they messed with El Cuco for a long time, but they didn't have any evidence against him. Neither my testimony nor Iván's helped them with that. A few months later, Iván went back to Mexico, and I moved. I think El Cuco also left the apartment because the rent went up and it didn't make sense for him to stay."

"Are you still in touch with them?"

"No. I don't know anything about their lives, and, truth be told, I don't give a shit."

"There's one last thing I want to ask you."

"Go on."

"Would you mind if I wrote about you and what you've told me?"

"That depends."

"On what?"

"Whether you're going to tell the truth or lie."

"I'm going to lie to create something true."

"Go ahead, then."

El Cuco Martínez, age 29. Hacker. Scener. Video game designer.

Room #3

He banged his sweaty palm on the door three times. He'd climbed nine floors, dodging needles, blood, empty bags, aluminum scraps, perforated cans, glass bottles, poems, and graffiti, abandoned junk on the stairs rechristened as "dump" in a building that was really called "home" for who knows how many squatters—most of them drug addicts—uninterested in reproducing the image of a sterile life, far from their truth of leftovers and trash. In this kind of place, El Cuco thought, kipple told a story of the underclass that revealed something meaningful in the garbage, in the indecipherable scribbles, and in the graffiti that versified punctured, pissed-on, shot-at walls with lines that said "EDUCATION IS THE STREET: LEARN TO WALK NAKED" or "JAIME DIED HERE WOUNDED AND WINDED AND WAS SHIPPED BACK TO THE BORDER." The dead artifact, he thought, transformed the world just as much as living artifacts, poems, and drawings. In that sense the needles were as poetic as the words written on the walls because, even though he wasn't sure what it was that others called poetry, he sensed the poem was the looking, not the letter.

/ /These are the lines from story A of *Nefando*,
Irene said,
and she also said: These are the lines from story B,
Españarri,
and these are from story C.

Montero opened the door while chewing on a bottle cap he then spit out—gnawed and covered in saliva—onto a table covered in food scraps. Annoyed, El Cuco looked around the little semi-empty, smelly living room where corners were covered in cobwebs, an endless line of ants climbed the kitchen wall, and flies swarmed the stove top. Was it hard to find the place? Montero asked as he flopped onto a haggard couch that immediately released a thick cloud of dust. Not too bad, he answered, then asked, feigning curiosity: Where's everyone else? Montero glanced down a short hallway to his right and stood up, weaving slightly. El Cuco unwillingly followed: his shoes stuck to the ground with every step he took, as if he were treading on gum. Prepare yourself, man, Montero told him, you're about to have the surprise of your fucking life, I'm telling you. El Cuco instinctively tensed the muscles in his arms when he caught sight of the Arab who'd deformed his face with a single blow three weeks before tied up and gagged in a windowless bedroom; the same guy who'd threatened and robbed him in broad daylight in an alley used by druggies and hookers. Fuck! he blurted as he watched the man panting in a corner, sweaty and furious, his arms, legs, and tongue immobilized. A dim light bulb swung like a pendulum, lengthening the shadows. In the middle of the room, Rubén and La Rata were regarding their prisoner with their arms crossed, shirtless, pacing the concrete space like two vermin in their lair. El Cuco noticed they both had bandaged hands. What do you think, tío? La Rata asked, baring a row of twisted black teeth. There was a lighter, a knife, and a bag of trash on the floor. What the fuck? El Cuco asked, disoriented. What the hell are you doing? he asked again, spreading his arms in the air, stretching out as if the room were suddenly closing in on him. Rubén, with a backward hat and deep greenish bags under his eyes, led him and Montero out of the room. The light in the hall was also dim and filtered through a tiny window that looked onto the building's interior. Rubén's reeking breath made El Cuco dizzy while he heard himself say: Shut your mouth, eh? Shut up because this has nothing to do with you, got it? Yesterday we burned down the Arab's father's fruit stand so he'd get the memo, he and the rest of his shitty group, that no Pakis are gonna scare us, much less tell us where we can work, you hear? El Cuco wheezed, confused, then yelled with his hands on his head: Fuck this bullshit, tío! Fuck this motherfucking bullshit! Fuck! Montero placed a hand on his shoulder like an axe: Calm down, Cuqui, calm down, we got it all planned out . . . As soon as we finish up with our friend in there, we'll get out of this pigsty and we'll be able to do whatever we want again, so relax, this is it, this is everything. But what the hell are you going to do to him? El Cuco demanded. Nothing, man, fuck . . . so you're gonna be a wuss, huh? Rubén said, spraying little droplets of spit on his face. We're gonna scare him, ok? That's it, so calm down and remember to shut your yap, you little bitch. You're a fucking son of a bitch, tío, I don't want any part of this, fuck, El Cuco said, pale and sweating as if in a sauna, with a mixture of rage and bewilderment. Why'd you ask me to come all the way down here, huh? I don't want any part of this, dammit. Why'd you ask me to come?

/ /Hey, Españarri, what do you think poetry is?
Irene said,
and she also said: Hey, Españarri, do you want me to recite a
slice of life?

We made you come, Rubén said, so you'd know what you're not gonna know, so chill out, ok? Because you don't know anything and you haven't seen anything, you're a fucking saint, ok? He smacked Montero on the back and commanded him: Give the kid his share so he settles down a bit, go on, let's see if that'll make him stop busting my balls for once. And he went back into the room with the calm of someone who has nothing to lose or fear or think. El Cuco stood there, his tongue tied and body burning, and when Montero led him back to the living room, all he could do was keep murmuring: Fuck, fuck this shit, fuck, in a ritornello that felt eternal. The shock was still distorting his facial features, but he tried to maintain a certain composure that would restore his lost calm. *Nefando* is like all writing: a telescope, Irene told him the night before when they talked about the project he'd agreed to take on. If he thought about Irene, revealer of complex, taciturn words, maybe everything else would disappear. Now other things mattered to him, he silently confessed, although he didn't know how to name them. Montero sat down on a chair with his legs spread wide and pulled four fifty-euro bills from a backpack abandoned on the floor and tossed them among the food scraps on the table. Here's your cut, Cuqui, he said. El Cuco took the money and quickly stuffed it in his pocket before any other disaster could stop him. He wanted to leave, but he didn't know how. The door was no longer a possible exit, and escaping from himself became an embarrassing aporia. Tell La Rata and Rubén, he gravely told Montero, that they're getting mixed up in some trouble they won't be able to get out of, OK, tell them I said they'd better let him go. And Montero yawned a stupid smile that eclipsed his attitude of disapproval. This is what I get for working with extremists, El Cuco thought as he made his way to the door and slammed it behind him, emphasizing his dissent.

/ /We never get bored,
Irene said,
and she also said: We look in the sand for the word "cloud"
and we look,
eternally—which isn't forever—
for a true expression of our own so we can understand ourselves.

Descending the stairs, a disquieting sensation still needling his palate, he saw written on the wall of the fifth floor:

MY HUNGER COMPETES IN THE RUINS WITH THE
FLITTING OF THIS FLY:

/ /What do you see?
Irene asked,
and she also asked: Tell me, what is the shape of your
ruins?

Interviewee: Iván Herrera

Location: Starbucks, Col. Hipódromo Condesa, 06100, Mexico City

"There are things you never forget, things you'll never understand, events you turn over and over in your head but stay as tightly shut as a locked box you left unopened at the opportune time for A or B reason. Then you clearly remember the surface of the box, you even dream about what could have been inside, but the contents, like it or not, are just a thousand and one assumptions you pull from the void. The recurring memories, the ones that stick with you, are like this: pieces that don't fit in personal puzzles, closed boxes, impenetrable bunkers . . . Everything else, everything that isn't a mystery even if it might partly be, is forgotten."

"Umm."

"What I can't forget about the Teráns, for example, is Cecilia. I don't think I ever talked to her for more than five minutes the entire time we were roommates. She was quiet, and I suspect she was a little crazy. She took tranquilizers, so yeah, I wouldn't say she was exactly healthy, really healthy. Once Kiki and I found her banging her head against the kitchen wall. It was like a scene from a horror movie. I'd heard a sound like fists banging from my room, but I never imagined . . . We managed to stop her, brought her to the room she shared with her siblings, and once we were all a little calmer, we realized she was slow, as if everything she saw was weighing down her eyes. I don't know why it scared me so much to see her like that, but I felt like a kid who isn't used to the world. I wasn't afraid for her, but of her. Her behavior, movement, and babbling made my hair stand on end. It sounds extremely selfish and dickish to say, but if Kiki hadn't been there, I would've left without giving a shit whether she split her head open. And I'm not a dick, güey, but that kind of situation always throws me off. I remember we found a bottle of tranquilizers in her things and asked if it was hers. It took her a long time to say yes because she was kinda out of it, like she was wearing a diving suit and listening to us from underwater. The medication was called Rivotril—I still remember it. The first thing, well the second thing we did was call her siblings to ask what to do, and Emilio told us not to do anything, they'd take care of everything, I mean Irene and him, obviously, so we stayed with Cecilia while the siblings headed back. Luckily she hadn't hurt herself too bad, or at least it didn't seem like she'd done much, but her whole forehead was swollen from banging her head so hard, so I thought she should go to the hospital, just to make sure there was no damage inside. That's what the siblings ended up doing because it seemed Cecilia had taken double the normal dose of Rivotril, which is what made her act like an idiot. But before Irene and Emilio got back, I remember sitting on the bed next to Cecilia reading the Rivotril medication guide, because back then I had no idea what that bullshit was, and I remember reading that it was for people with epilepsy or panic attacks, and truth be told, I was really fucking surprised, though I don't know why, since I didn't know anything about her life. Well, I did know about her relationship with her siblings, but that wasn't enough. Anyone sharing such a small apartment would have figured that out, especially since none of them tried to hide it. They didn't care if we knew, which was fine. That was their business, and I never judged them, you know, because I didn't give a shit about their sex lives. I try to live my life without judging or singling anyone else out. It's what I'd like others to do with me: ignore me and not impose their moral codes or private rules or force me to exist in their own cults. In any case, I was there, sitting on the bed next to Cecilia, who hadn't said a word until then, who hadn't moved or looked at anyone, and she put her jellyfish-like hand on my arm and looked into my eyes, hers suddenly clear and relaxed, and I got scared, obviously, but then she said in a fragile little voice 'Colon,' and I yelled for Kiki, who'd gone to the bathroom, but she didn't come. I don't know if she even heard me. I actually thought

Cecilia was delirious until she said 'The colon is used to call attention to what's yet to come,' which made a lot more sense than the other thing, so I started paying attention to what she was saying. There are things I've forgotten, but not the closed boxes. I remember she said, 'As if there were a colon in front. Do you see my landscape?'"

"And what does that mean?

"Well, I don't know, güey. How the hell am I supposed to know what that means? Maybe she was telling me to pay attention to something, or maybe she was saying it to herself. I don't know what landscape she was talking about. What I do know is that, for some reason, just as her siblings arrived, she said, in front of them, sounding really riled up: 'They aren't me.' And then she didn't say anything else, because they took her to the hospital. When she returned, she was pretty much back to normal, though she said she remembered everything that happened and everything she said. According to Irene there was a mix-up with the grams in the Rivotril capsules and that's why Cecilia, who apparently got panic attacks, had acted like a crazy person: because of the excess Rivotril in her system, they said the doctors said. I believe them because Cecilia never behaved like that again, so I guess it was all a consequence of taking more than the prescribed dose, but I kept thinking about what she'd told me when she was out of it, and one night when I found her alone, luckily, because her siblings were always prowling around, making it almost impossible to talk to any of them one-on-one, I seized my chance to go back to what happened that day. I tried to be casual, just to see what she'd say, and Cecilia, who never smiled, smiled at me and confessed she remembered having thought, while banging her head against the wall, that her body wasn't a temple. She told me she tirelessly repeated the sentence 'My body is not a temple' and that she felt the need, no, the urgency, to prove that what that voice bellowed at her from a perfect omniscience, inhabiting her, stripping her naked, was true. 'It made sense. Only thus could I free myself of the sacred, and the sacred, in that moment, repulsed me,' she said. And I think I understood her better than she could have imagined, better than whatever you might be imagining right now, güey. Because very few

people in this world want, even just once in their life, to reduce themselves to their merest expression, the one we fall into through physical
pain, through the ultimate revelation of our fragility, through how
easy it is for us to break down, through the instability and mutability
we all are."

"And you've wanted that yourself? Don't tell me you banged your
head on a wall."

"We all bang our heads on a wall, we just don't realize and write
it off as an accident. But no, güey, I only write about complex things,
like you."

"And you don't think she might have said that because she knew it
would be deeply meaningful for you? Because it seems strange to me,
I don't know if you agree, that a person so drugged up would have
such profound thoughts about their body."

"Yes, it's possible. Maybe she knew things about me that I hadn't
noticed. That's one of the closed boxes, but I don't understand why
Cecilia would want to tell me something like that only to forge a con-
nection she wouldn't use for anything else later, because we never
talked about anything important ever again. I think what emerged in
her that day with the Rivotril was something she already had inside
her, and maybe she'd been developing those thoughts you call profound for a long time. In any case, that's the end of my story about
Cecilia Terán and the beginning of the question: What did she mean
by 'a colon,' 'they aren't me,' and 'do you see my landscape?' The
answer could be nothing. But there could also be something there. In
fact, I think there is something. Because the Teráns, because of what
happened to them as kids, tried to say things."

"You and El Cuco and Kiki never question the truthfulness of
what happened to the Teráns, but how can you be so sure that the
kids in those videos are really them?"

"Am I absolutely sure it was them, well, no. But I believe it. I really
believe it."

The Hype Pornovela Library

CHAPTER THREE
By Kiki Ortega

I

The blood on Nella's skin: there are very few images like blood on skin. Diego and Eduardo felt a wave so intense and red, so much of the sea inside them, bubbling in their bellies when they looked at her, when she put them in her eyes swollen with the school of God's fish—a divine plague, a legendary grouping—fish with teeth swimming in the desires of the ossuaries and of the angular stones they monumentalized on their tongues. Red bridges appeared like the bloody skin: red pupils, red fingers, Nella's scabbed red nails on the grass; and her skin so moonshiny beneath the dust of life; and the mystery buried beneath the well of her skin. They traveled liquidly toward that daybreak as she dug into her flesh and sighed:

SCATTER ME HERE

OVER THIS NAMELESS DEATH

And she was already mourning her tomorrow.

II

Ever since they had discovered the animal in the depths of Nella, always open and dangerous like the forest's jawbone, Diego and Eduardo sought to embed her in their silences and nocturnal rituals with an urgency born from admiration and estrangement. They unnostalgically abandoned their seats in the middle of the classroom to settle on either side of her in the back row during the classes as Nella just flipped through the pages of a battered anatomy book. Magnanimous, she let them get closer but ignored them as if she were doing them a favor by admitting them into her space, an invisible circle that both defined and expanded her. The outlook improved when, during a long recess, they returned her camera by way of an apology. Nella then deigned to look at them and proffer monosyllabic responses to their questions; a step forward that opened a path of brief but effective communication among the three. Diego and Eduardo showed her their comics, their books, their exemplary novellas, and she showed them her folder with old illustrations of dissected animals and drawings she'd done of bodies called "death throes." Nella's pleasures, which involved the most hidden part of the self, that which has no name, something as mystical as discontinuity and a scream spreading inside only to shoot out into the world, awoke in Diego and Eduardo a dull, earthy desire that existed in their skin but sunk into the current of silence.

"Let us come with you one night," they asked.

Nella closed her eyes.

III

One day, for no particular reason, the literature teacher wrote on the chalkboard:

D

E

U

IS

I

L

E

N

C

E

IV

Night fell. Diego and Eduardo pursued Nella's footsteps toward the forest without a word, maintaining the distance she'd ordered they keep, respecting the circle around her, while the cats of the security guard, who was dozing in a chair by the lake, followed the smell of tuna on Nella's hands. Little by little, the foliage started to swallow and blind them until their eyes were reborn in the dark nature: a mirrored vision of shadows fallen like stalks bent toward the ground. They stopped in the same clearing where they'd trapped her two weeks before, knowing this time that had never happened; they'd never caught her nor could they. Five hungry cats with vast, sun-gleaming gazes prowled around for several minutes, but only the youngest let Nella touch it and licked her tuna-streaked fingers, happy and unaware that it had been chosen. She petted it, and Diego and Eduardo, very still next to a twisted trunk, watched her feed the kitten with a tenderness that made them think, in spite of everything, that her actions showed love and respect for animals. The other cats ran away, disappointed, when Nella placed the last chunk of tuna into a clear plastic bag, but the chosen one, the most trusting, naively walked into the trap from which it would never emerge. The cat was surprised to realize—too late—that the hand that had fed it was the same one sealing the bag. Clumsy as it was, Diego thought, the struggle of the animal flopping around on the ground was dignified. The yowls sounded far away, as if the battle were being waged somewhere else, and Nella sat down on the ground, engrossed in the sight of this wild desperation to survive, and turned on her camera. Diego and Eduardo didn't know how much time passed as she looked at and occasionally photographed the animal, which was starting to suffocate. It wasn't the death in and of itself, they understood, that made the hair on Nella's arm stand on end or dampened her face: it was the process by which something was extinguished once it had spit out, furious, the full force of its desire to remain. When the bag stopped moving, Diego and Eduardo felt, deep in some recess of themselves, the flutter of the chosen cat's death rattle. Nella trembled. For a few seconds, the silence was perfect.

Then she pulled out a knife.

She delicately extracted the cat from the bag and placed it on the ground as her equal. When she slit the belly open, the blood spilled like a storm in her barely blinking eyes. Diego and Eduardo realized, before the thunder, that the forest was its heartbeat and they'd never lived this way. Nella smiled from afar, panting, as she plunged her right hand into the guts of the chosen body, the epicenter of heats and white abysses, north of all roads. Diego and Eduardo were aroused by her arousal, her sweat, her joy, but they didn't do anything, fearing they'd disrupt the moment. Intuition told them the night was solemn and they were invisible, pieces of a monochrome stage where the protagonist was Nella and her quest. They struggled to contain their drives when she brought her bloody hand under her skirt and started touching herself while looking up at the sky. Her sighs illuminated thousands of leaves.

> The cat penetrated the earth.

V

Words can't say that words can't say, Nella once told them, that's what my "death throes" are for.

VI

In one of his exemplary novellas, Eduardo made Wanda and O meet in a Gothic castle, though neither really knew why or how they'd ended up there. They dine together at a table set with food for them, and under the light of just a couple of candelabras, they talk about their condition as characters in erotic novels. Wanda complains that she hasn't been able to deploy her true ingenuity; that she hasn't been satisfied by reaching the limit, much less surpassing it, in *Venus in Furs,* while O says she is happy with the ending the author of her story had granted her desire; that is, she'd exhausted it, wrung it out until the destruction that was, of course, death: the greatest orgasm. Once they finish discussing the importance of the idea behind total possession or total surrender, about the dissolution of the *I* or the onomastic *I,* the only really nameable one, the pair goes down to the castle's dungeon, following the directions of a raccoon, and find Erzsébet Báthory. Hanging from the ceiling on the orders of the countess, with thick chains around their wrists, a dozen girls who are bleeding profusely and writhing, still alive, with pain. Carved into their flesh are names like Justine, Marcela, Mother, María, Kitty, Jane, Clarissa, Monique, etc. In the end, Wanda, O, and Erzsébet lick the blood from her victims' bodies and perform oral sex before killing them.

"What did you think?" Eduardo asked Nella when she set the pages aside.

"It would have been better with boys and horses."

VII

Nella's first time was everything they'd imagined and nothing she'd imagined. It happened in the forest, one moonless, starless night, black as her hair and her lizard eyes, with the ever-present noise of the insects repopulating themselves and the hooting of an owl. Diego and Eduardo undressed while she watched with an expression branching out into questions she didn't ask. Their bodies surrounded her, though not to threaten her this time, and they slowly removed her uniform, cautiously, somewhat nervously revealing her. At first Nella seemed reluctant to let them look at her, but when they saw her naked, they understood by her trembling that she wasn't used to being observed or caressed by others, and that her distrust was, like everyone's, related to the unknown. They looked at her carefully and found her to be fragile and immature, so different from her interior; they smelled her, touched her, and kissed her all over, but the first to penetrate her was Eduardo, the gentler of the two. Nella didn't scream, didn't moan: she just bit her lip and winced when Diego entered her, and despite the roughness of his railing, she stayed quiet.

A few hours later, as they got dressed, Nella said that next time she wanted them to kill a really big animal together.

VIII

One afternoon Nella read a poem by Alejandra Pizarnik and decided it was erotic:

DAYBREAK
Naked and dreaming of a solar night.
I've lain through animal days.
The wind and the rain erased me
as they might a fire, or a poem
written on a wall.
(TR. YVETTE SIEGERT)

For days she repeated, "I've lain through animal days."
"I've lain through animal days."
　　　　"I've lain through animal days."
　　　　　　　　"I've lain through animal days."
Diego and Eduardo embraced that idea.

IX

In the eleventh chapter of *The Digressions of the Succubus Poet,* the succubus visits Eduardo's mom and convinces her to sleep with her son. After understanding that only thus, by violating the taboo, could she ever be free from herself, the mother walks to the son's room, finds him asleep in bed, gets naked, and climbs on top of him. Eduardo wakes up enveloped in caresses and, of course, does nothing to move away from his mother, from his erect penis, from its rosy color. Over fifteen vignettes, the two have furious sex on a creaking bed while the succubus watches intently from a corner, taking an inactive role in the comic for the first time. When the mother finally reaches the coveted orgasm, she falls dead to the ground, and Eduardo, still full of energy, transforms into a hermaphrodite with enormous genitals. The succubus applauds the metamorphosis and recites these lines in the final vignette: "You ate from your mother: / now you can climb the mountains."

X

What they want to see is what Nella sees when her eyes shine with the blood of a dying creature or with death itself, always overwhelming, planting itself in the flesh reaper's open palm.

What she wants is for them to see what she sees when her skin bristles and her mind splits.

What she sees is

　　　　．
　　　　．

XI

The big animal had to be the black horse that grazed on them.

XII

Knowing there was no turning back, they spilled the blood of their bodies onto the earth, and the earth sucked up their blood, and it was as if they became themselves again, as if they returned to the source and opened up to the passion, the disintegration of the ONE—origin of all horrors—while Nella watched them, beloved, fallen onto the pile of rocky life, impenetrable, they said, but there they were, entering it with their blood awakened, never again caged, and fear was a sunward pyramid they didn't see, only their lizard eyes, their eyes crying in the cold that made them sweat against the earth and pulled them closer and suctioned them to the source, to kilometer zero, to the submission for which they weren't yet ready, and then they demanded, drenched in their blood, "Show us how to be your animals." And Nella licked her gums and plunged her knife, cutting the lamb but not the horse, so that Diego and Eduardo would understand what not to do: degrade the mystery.

"This is the sand dune in every erotic story," Nella said.

"No," they said, "this is the dune in our foreheads."

Epilogue to "The Hype Pornovela Library"

Here I put an end to the word

I, the writer:

the only character.

EXHIBITION OF MY RUINS
María Cecilia Terán, age 14.

box

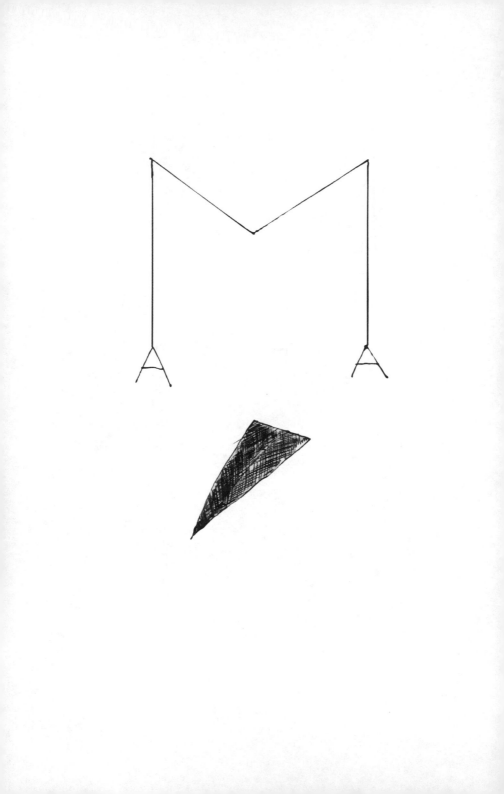

DESCRIBE

TU

desgarramiento

DESCRIBE *Your ripping*

DESCRIBE

ESGARRAMiENTO

TU

DESCRIBE YOUR RIPPING

Mi desgarramiento

es

como

My ripping is like

Mi Desgarramiento

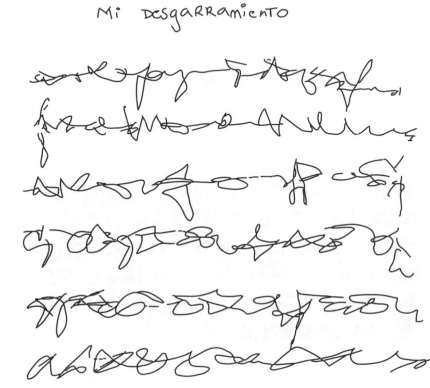

My ripping

mi

voz

My voice

INFANCIA

Y

Childhood and

Mi paisaje
:

My landscape:

C X J A Y J E Q T E Q S
C J A B Q A V C C E X P N
E B B Q E Ñ V C O T A S L K A
S A Z C P C O R W M B D C F
P L F R D O C J V F R Y F
B W S K T S N A D J S H
Z J Q X N R U X L T W K T
U X J L H C G H X Y Q E M
B X D I R G S E Q Z Y L
N J T K Ñ A D B P J O L
G F U T X S D O P C V G S N
G R C Y S D X N X D A Q
Q T V B B L X T K J
X J D A B N X Z T F V N R A
J D A F V

Interviewee: El Cuco Martínez

Location: Sor Rita Bar, Carrer de la Mercè 27, 08002, Barcelona

"One night there was a blackout in the whole neighborhood and we were stuck in the dark for five hours. We didn't even have candles or flashlights. We were like the newly blind, bumping into furniture and tripping over things strewn across the floor, because we were never especially neat, let me tell you, and that's how it was until our eyes adjusted and we could more or less see with the moon coming in through the window, right? A moon so pale that it distorted the scene and transformed everything into shadows like in Plato's cave. All six of us were home, and we were sweating balls. God it was so hot! It was August or September, I dunno, but the apartment was a sauna, tío, and all six of us were there, in the heat, like moles, pff! When the power went out, you could hear shouts all around the building because half the neighborhood was watching a soccer match and was pissed about the outage. I was in my room with Irene, talking about *Nefando* and fine-tuning details you wouldn't understand, and then we came out . . . Man, don't get offended, Jesus, it's just programming stuff, that's what I mean, it has nothing to do with how smart you are. Man, please. As I was saying, we both came out to see what was going on and then walked with the others to the windows, feeling our way with our hands, to see the whole neighborhood turned off, looking like an enormous cardboard model, unrecognizable, something you'd hide in the back of a closet. Then Irene and I went back into my room, I don't know why, and we lay down on my bed, or rather she lay down and I sat, as if the mattress weren't mine, fuck. I was intimidated by the way that tía took over everything. It was like the world belonged to her, and you had to ask permission to touch

157

any object around her. She didn't do it on purpose, of course, that's just how she was. Some people are so totally in command of themselves that they become the center of every space, you know what I mean? In short, we chatted for a bit about some things I've forgotten by now, but I do remember I was worried Emilio would turn up. I don't know why, if we weren't doing anything wrong, but I was nervous because he was there that night, in the living room or another room, and he could misinterpret Irene and me being alone together, on my bed, in the dark, because like it or not, being on the same bed in the dark is intimate. I won't deny I was attracted to her, but nothing ever happened between us. I dunno. All I remember is what came after she asked about my mother. No. Wait. She didn't ask about my mother, that's not what happened. She asked about my worst childhood memory. Awful things happen to all of us when we're kids, she said, but sometimes we forget them or they don't seem that bad once we grow up. I couldn't see her well, I mean the night had blurred her face, but she said it as if she no longer thought the things they did to her were all that bad. I liked the cynicism she had with herself. She was lost, tío, like all of us, but she rejoiced in the awareness of being lost, you know? She wasn't looking for a way to smile at herself. She didn't have that sick obsession with the future that most people do. She preferred to live her now. And that was cool, tío. Though maybe I'm wrong in this description of her, I dunno. And it's not like I really got to know her, like you get to know a friend. Sometimes I go off the rails and end up talking bullshit, sorry. I dunno, in any case, what did the world of childhood represent for them. I mean the siblings, of course. The way they had of looking at the past, after what their asshole father did to them, it's beyond me. I'll never be able to understand it. Words aren't enough for everything inside someone, but it's all we have, and that's why we try to say everything, isn't it? Which reminds me of a conversation I had with the youngest Terán, Cecilia. I think her siblings were there. She told me something like, silence isn't the absence of speaking or of writing, but the instant when words lose all meaning. She really insisted that true silence occurs when two or more people are speaking, that is, right as they're doing it, in the very act that's supposedly the antithesis of silence, not when they're quiet. For example, it could happen now, between you and me, with no pause in the conversation. Or at least I think that's what she said. I dunno. The tía was a bit unhinged, but she wasn't stupid. The night of the blackout I told Irene about an episode from my childhood that I'd forgotten or at least repressed in hopes of forgetting. Telling it meant remembering it, breaking my own silence, so it was fine, I guess. I'll tell you because I feel like I can be open with you now. One afternoon, when I was six or so, my mother took me for a walk. Back then she'd already started to suffer rough episodes from her illness, I don't know if I told you my mother has a disorder, well, she's obsessive compulsive, you know what I mean? She gets depressed, repeats everything she does three times, groups everything in threes, and so on. There were days when I had to stay at my uncle's because she'd disappear, and when she finally turned up again, she'd do weird stuff and not listen to anyone. I don't know if you've ever looked into the face of a person who's out of their mind, but I'm telling you it's just like Munch's painting, and it's so scary you shit yourself because you know, when you see that face, there's no way to predict what that person will do or what their limits are. It's important to know these peoples' limits, tío, because, fuck, if you think about it, that's what makes us able to relate to others. Anyway, that afternoon I was really happy because it seemed like things were getting better and because we were taking a walk together, getting out of the house, and I was going to run around and maybe get an ice cream or play in a park with normal kids. She smiled at me, just a little, but at least she no longer had that dilated expression she had when she looked at me for years, until I had the balls to leave her, because you can't live like that, let me tell you. I remember she got me dressed and tied my shoelaces. She also held my hand. We walked for a long time. The sky was red. We were crossing a bridge when I realized my fly was down, so I zipped it up, giggling. Then my mother stopped to look at the sunset and leaned on the railing, you know, with her elbows on the bar and her hands around her jawbone, like something out of a rom-com. I remember I tried to do the same thing, but I was too little to lean, I could only grab the lower bars, which forced me to see the sky all slashed by black lines. I don't know if I fussed, I don't think so, but I might have. Anyway, how can I trust my own memory? What's more likely is that the sky wasn't red but orange, and that my mother hadn't leaned there in such a cheesy way, but how would you know? I can only know what I remember. My mother looked at me and asked if I wanted a better look at the sky, and of course I said yes. She lifted me into the air and sat me down on the railing. I don't understand how no one stopped to say, Hey, ma'am, that's dangerous, you can't have your little boy sitting on the edge of the abyss! I was a smart kid and immediately realized something was wrong. Nothing had happened, but my mother's face suddenly wasn't the same, you know what I'm saying? Her features started to crumple like when she'd have her episodes. I was so scared I grabbed her arms and asked her to put me down. Then something happened that my mother always denied. She smiled and leaned me backward, toward the void, and told me she was going to let go. I started to cry, of course, and clung on to her even tighter. I think I hurt her, but she never stopped smiling, and that would have been fine if it weren't for her eyes, which were like two used ashtrays, tío, what do I know; they were two endless corridors, or no, more like, you know what they were like? Bunny nests. Yes, bleak like that. And I knew she wasn't playing. I don't know how, but I knew it. I mean, you can sense danger just like any other animal: your hair stands on end, your heart races, you can't breathe, and then you know you're fucked. She didn't let go, of course, because here I am, but she wanted to and that's really hard for a kid: to know his mother wanted to hurt him. You see, for some of us the hostility of the world starts at home, you know what I'm saying? There are little devastations that shape you early on. I dunno. The moment you lose trust . . . That moment changes you, and nothing's ever the same after that. Let's say what happens in the dark stays in the dark and multiplies, but it never dies. It must be something like that. What do you want me to say? My trust in the world has its wrinkles and grooves, but Irene's . . . Irene trusted her distrust and believed that would save her from the past.

Or that's how it seemed to me. I dunno, I dunno. She once told me that when someone's world is destroyed, nothing is left, not even the pain, because pain can only exist when there's still a world. Sometimes we talked about that, about how there's an important difference between collapse and destruction. A collapsed world can get back up if it's able to explain the void, the desert, but a destroyed world can do nothing but reconstruct itself, and reconstruction means making something new on top of the ruins. So the destroyed world is a dead world, get it? No, no, I'm not gonna drink anything else. But listen, tío, this is the best part. I was there, opening up to Irene, telling her what I remembered, or remembering what I was telling, very comfortable in my space, or at least feeling calm in all that darkness, because I knew what was around me, when the door suddenly opened and guess who came in? No? Well, you're gonna be shocked when I tell you, tío, because it's worthy of a horror film, because ultimately that's how all revelations are: terrifying. No idea, huh? You'll never guess. I don't think I've ever been more scared in my fucking life, holy shit, but the person who came in was the person I least expected. If E.T. himself had pushed open my bedroom door with his fucking glowing finger, I would've been less surprised than when I recognized, from the faint light in the hall, Irene's silhouette in the shadows, and her voice, tío, her voice that I thought was unmistakable, saying something I can't remember anymore. Fuck. Who the hell had I been talking to, then? That's the big question, tío. Ha! Irene came into my room, and in a matter of milliseconds everything was absolute uncertainty. No, worse than that, tío: it was my certainty of the broken world, shattered to pieces in my hands. And all I could do was jump out of bed and look at the person I'd been talking to for over half an hour, but really look at her, for the first time, with the faint light from the sky stretching down the hall and seeping in, and I couldn't believe it, but I saw Emilio; fucking Emilio Terán, goddammit! I know it sounds unbelievable, tío, like a bad story with a dramatic ending, but this isn't a story or the ending I want to tell you. And the truth is, even though I can't explain it or understand how it happened, I didn't realize I'd been talking to Emilio and not Irene.

I was out of my mind for several minutes, of course, and the siblings tried to calm me down, and they eventually did. Apparently, when I went out with Irene to the living room because the power went out, she'd separated from me, and the person who came back into the bedroom was her brother. Emilio and I got along pretty well, I mean it wasn't strange that he'd come up to me and we'd end up shooting the shit, but what I hadn't noticed was the change, I hadn't heard the difference between Emilio's and Irene's voices for that whole time, voices that did sound totally different once I realized what was going on, I hadn't noticed the obvious differences between the silhouette of a man and a woman, despite the dark, I hadn't even sensed something weird about the conversation, something that might make me think, Irene wouldn't say that—well, tío, it all really messed with me, I'm not gonna lie. It was as if I suddenly realized that's the state of the human mind before knowledge. We believe we know, we believe what we know is true and objective, and later, like a hurricane ripping trees out of the ground, we realize our certainties were founded on misunderstandings and all that's left is the desolation, the sinking ship, the anxiety before the emptiness that makes it impossible for you to rely on your perceptions or on your ideas of things. If that isn't fear, what else could it be? OK, sure, I wouldn't mind another beer. Fuck, tío, I know what you're trying to do, I know you want to get me drunk. It's not like I hadn't thought about this stuff before, but it isn't the same to think about it as it is to experience it so vividly, you know what I'm saying? We're always in the dark, tío, always: that's the conclusion. Afterward, Irene, Emilio, and I went out into the living room and joined Kiki, Iván, and Cecilia, who were on the sofa talking about who knows what, but I couldn't stop thinking about my error the whole time we sat there in the shadows. I dunno. I still can't explain how I got them mixed up. I failed to notice the change because I was sure I knew who I was talking to. Do you think I tricked myself or simply stopped looking? If we can't trust in our certainties, tío, there's no ground for any of us to stand on. Sometimes it feels like everything around me is water and I'm in the middle of that ocean, far from any shore. It's a feeling of exhaustion, but I can't let myself sink. Every passing day is full of hours I spend swimming toward the nothingness. And it's always the same horizon: an absurd line imitating a morning that doesn't really exist. Beyond the horizon is just another empty horizon: that's all I know. I remember Cecilia started talking about some sci-fi novels I'd lent her. The Teráns were the opposite of science fiction because they looked backward to see the present. I don't think the horizon existed for any of them, though Irene once told me, 'I look forward to the time when all parents eat their children.' Like Chronos, you know what I'm saying, who by swallowing his children swallowed the morning and all the days that followed in order to perpetuate himself. Swallowing the parents, on the other hand, is the natural thing: it's communion, not parricide. It isn't the desire to perpetuate yourself, it's the only possible way of being born. Iván asked, 'How the hell do you eat your parents?' And Emilio answered, 'By taking away the only thing they have: their authority.' Back then I didn't know anything about the videos or the siblings' past, but when I found out, questions swirled in my head. I never understood, for example, why they didn't want to take revenge on their father, when it was clear they detested him. Maybe they hated him, I don't know, that surely would've been the normal thing, but nothing was normal with them. I once told Irene that what that man had done to them was a monstrosity, and she looked at me like I was a child. 'He's a man, not a monster,' she said, and I understood what she was saying so clearly that I never brought it up again. Do you get what she was trying to tell me? Well, tío, that they weren't victims of a monstrosity, but of a humanity. An abject humanity that all of us suffer in our flesh and mind, with variations, of course, but in the end we're connected by the same dark, chaotic nature of a mythical character, and the paradox is that this nexus always brings us back to the same place: uncertainty. I dunno, I dunno. I remember there was a moment when we didn't say anything, not Kiki, not Iván, not the siblings, not me. I don't think that was the silence. We could barely see each other's faces, and all the windows were open, but outside I heard only crickets, the world seemed to have been turned off too, and I felt safe in the company of strangers and in being one myself. After all, what did I know about the consciousnesses in front of me? What did I know about my own consciousness? And the most terrible thing was sensing that I was like those shadows, anchored in a continuous present, without any expectations, without any tomorrow, just that cave, right? The question is: Do you think there are words for this darkness? I imagine you have an opinion, and now's a good time to say it. Are there words for all the silence yet to come?"

Translator's Note

The deeply disturbing *Nefando* in large part launched Mónica Ojeda's literary career, earning her a spot on the 2017 Bogotá39 list of emerging young writers. It was through this list that I first found Ojeda's work, as I was drawn to the description of a novel about a controversial video game. In its original Spanish version, *Nefando* has had a major impact in Spain and Latin America because its intimate, brutally original portrait of the fears and desires of a group of young artists living in Barcelona.

In the novel, *Nefando*, or the journey into the bowels of a room, is a little-known online game that was quickly deleted because of its controversial and sensitive content. The experiences of its players became the center of gamer debates on forums within the deepest corners of the web. The users seem unable to come to an agreement— was it a horror game for geeks, a staging of immorality, or a poetic exercise? Were the bowels of that room as deep and twisted as they seemed? In the novel, six young people share an apartment in Barcelona, their rooms vibrating like hives. In each private room, disturbing and murky activities take place: the writing of a pornographic novel, the frustrated desire for self-castration, or the development of designs for the demo scene, the artistic subculture of the digital world. Through these acts, the characters explore the territories of their bodies, their minds, and their childhoods.

Nefando the novel is composed of interviews, journal entries, the beginnings of a novel, online forum discussions, and drawings that work together to create a portrait of these six characters. The reader is first introduced to Kiki Ortega, a young writer from Mexico who has received a FONCA grant to live and write in Barcelona; she is writing a pornographic novel, and many of the chapters dedicated to her are either a textual manifestation of her writing process or excerpts from a draft of her novel. Kiki's compatriot, Iván Herrera, is also a writer, in Barcelona for a master's program in creative writing. His monologues, written in the second person, reveal a deeply conflicted relationship with his own flesh and a desire to have a woman's body. El Cuco Martínez, a video-game designer, is the only Spaniard in the novel. Within the apartment, he seems to have had an intermediary role among the six—and he is the one to design and implement *Nefando*. Sexually abused by their father as children, the final three characters—the Ecuadorian Terán siblings, Irene, Emilio, and Cecilia—are largely silent throughout the novel, but it is they who came up with the ideas behind *Nefando*.

Ojeda skillfully reproduces the linguistic tendencies that differentiate the geographic background of these characters, thus creating a polyphonic text. Many readers have already pointed out the echoes of Bolaño in the way that an unidentified detective interviews the various characters, attempting to reach some sort of truth about the disturbing video game that garnered such a cult following. Reading this novel is intense, as the narrative endeavors to make the reader uncomfortable by openly showing the perverse, the abject, and the violent in an attempt to understand the pain of others.

This novel is not for the faint of heart; it deals with serious issues such as anxiety, body dysmorphia, pedophilia, child pornography, incest, and self-mutilation. There were chapters that were deeply unsettling for me to spend extended time with as I translated them. This is precisely the point of the novel—Ojeda asks her reader to confront the violence and brutality of the world, to think about what we do with that fear and evil. For the characters in this novel, creativity in the form of video-game design, creative writing, and visual art becomes a tool to deal with trauma, restructuring that trauma and flipping the role of victim. This refusal to be victimized—seen especially clearly in the way the Terán siblings articulate their childhood experiences in conversations and video-game design—is especially powerful. As a translator and reader, however, it is often difficult to stay immersed in a painful world, even one that is created through beautiful and inventive language. There were times I had to separate myself from the difficult passages by giving myself permission to work on something else or not work at all.

In an essay for *Words Without Borders*, Lara Vergnaud writes beautifully about translating trauma as she reflects on her work with Franck Bouysse's *Of No Woman Born*—how she avoided and finally worked her way into the difficult passages. At a loss for an approach that would really protect the translator from the pain, Vergnaud concludes that "the grim truth is that translating the pain and terror on the page may be preferable to what's out in the world. The page, at least, gives us space to prepare, to delay as long as needed. And so, my recommended mechanism is this: amid the darkness, try to stay, if not in the light, then at least in shadow."[1] This really resonates with my experience translating this novel.

On the more technical side of things, one major challenge of this translation was to recreate the differentiated character voices in both narrative chapters and interviews. Part of this task entailed listening to the language and paying attention to each character's tendencies in sentence length, use of slang and profanities, pronoun choice, etc. El Cuco, for instance, constantly repeats in Spanish, "No sé, no sé," which in English became, "I dunno, I dunno." Here and in other places throughout the novel, these repeated phrases reinforce a particular character's voice as well as their insecurities and unanswered questions. Furthermore, the language the characters use overtly reflects regional differences in Spanish. These characters also come from different parts of the Spanish-speaking world; El Cuco is Spanish, Kiki and Iván are Mexican, and the three Terán siblings are Ecuadorian. I did keep one linguistic tag in Spanish to tie a character to their place of origin, as Ojeda was doing the same thing when she played with regional uses of language. I maintain El Cuco's use of

---

1. Lara Vergnaud, "Translating (in) Darkness," *Words Without Borders*, June 10, 2020, https://wordswithoutborders.org/read/article/2020-06/translating-in-darkness-lara-vergnaud/.

tía and *tío*—literally "aunt" and "uncle," these terms are used by the Spanish to refer to peers. For the Mexican characters, I maintained the use of *guey*, which is used in much the same way as the Spanish *tío/tía*. These language tags at least gesture to the culturally specific and distinct voices Ojeda created.

One other linguistic consideration I made relates to the title: whether to keep it as is, or to translate it into something that might get at the same idea while still evoking a video game. While I considered titles such as *The Unspeakable*, *The Odious*, or *The Nefarious*, I ultimately retained *Nefando*. I felt that for an English-language reader, this title would bring to mind words such as *nefarious* while retaining a sense of the darkness and evil expressed in a term that is already somewhat rare in Spanish.

Translating Mónica Ojeda's writing continues to stretch my linguistic creativity and literary sensibilities in wonderful and frightening ways. I am deeply grateful to Coffee House Press for their continued support of Ojeda's work, and to Lizzie Davis for her editorial expertise. Robin Myers beautifully edited my translation; I so appreciated having her alongside me to wrestle with the difficult images. My wonderful translation workshop of Julia Sanches, Natascha Bruce, and Heather Houde offered excellent insight into excerpts and helped me make some of the bigger translation decisions in the book. Thank you, too, to my friend Jeff Pool, for helping me untangle the programming language; and, of course, to my wonderful husband, Bob Noffsinger, for always entertaining (and engaging with) my constant translation questions. Finally, I am tremendously grateful to Mónica Ojeda for entrusting me and the amazing team at Coffee House Press with another project.

—Sarah Booker
Morganton, North Carolina

Coffee House Press began as a small letterpress operation in 1972 and has grown into an internationally renowned nonprofit publisher of literary fiction, essay, poetry, and other work that doesn't fit neatly into genre categories.

Coffee House is both a publisher and an arts organization. Through our *Books in Action* program and publications, we've become inter-disciplinary collaborators and incubators for new work and audience experiences. Our vision for the future is one where a publisher is a catalyst and connector.

LITERATURE
is not the same thing as
PUBLISHING

Funder Acknowledgments

Coffee House Press is an internationally renowned independent book publisher and arts nonprofit based in Minneapolis, MN; through its literary publications and *Books in Action* program, Coffee House acts as a catalyst and connector—between authors and readers, ideas and resources, creativity and community, inspiration and action.

Coffee House Press books are made possible through the generous support of grants and donations from corporations, state and federal grant programs, family foundations, and the many individuals who believe in the transformational power of literature. This activity is made possible by the voters of Minnesota through a Minnesota State Arts Board Operating Support grant, thanks to the legislative appropriation from the Arts and Cultural Heritage Fund. Coffee House also receives major operating support from the Amazon Literary Partnership, Jerome Foundation, Literary Arts Emergency Fund, McKnight Foundation, and the National Endowment for the Arts (NEA). To find out more about how NEA grants impact individuals and communities, visit www.arts.gov.

Coffee House Press receives additional support from Bookmobile; the Buckley Charitable Fund; Dorsey & Whitney LLP; the Gaea Foundation; the Matching Grant Program Fund of the Minneapolis Foundation; Mr. Pancks' Fund in memory of Graham Kimpton; the Schwab Charitable Fund; and the U.S. Bank Foundation.

The Publisher's Circle of Coffee House Press

Publisher's Circle members make significant contributions to Coffee House Press's annual giving campaign. Understanding that a strong financial base is necessary for the press to meet the challenges and opportunities that arise each year, this group plays a crucial part in the success of Coffee House's mission.

Recent Publisher's Circle members include many anonymous donors, Kathy Arnold, Patricia A. Beithon, Andrew Brantingham, Kelli & Dave Cloutier, Theodore Cornwell, Mary Ebert & Paul Stembler, Kamilah Foreman, Eva Galiber, Jocelyn Hale & Glenn Miller Charitable Fund of the Minneapolis Foundation, Roger Hale & Nor Hall, Randy Hartten & Ron Lotz, Carl & Heidi Horsch, Amy L. Hubbard & Geoffrey J. Kehoe Fund of the St. Paul & Minnesota Foundation, Kenneth & Susan Kahn, the Kenneth Koch Literary Estate, Cinda Kornblum, the Lenfestey Family Foundation, Sarah Lutman & Rob Rudolph, Carol & Aaron Mack, Gillian McCain, Mary & Malcolm McDermid, Daniel N. Smith III & Maureen Millea Smith, Robin Chemers Neustein, Vance Opperman, Alan Polsky, Robin Preble, Steve Smith, Paul Thissen, Grant Wood, and Margaret Wurtele.

For more information about the Publisher's Circle and other ways to support Coffee House Press books, authors, and activities, please visit www.coffeehousepress.org/pages/donate or contact us at info@coffeehousepress.org.

Mónica Ojeda is the author of the novels *La desfiguración Silva* (Premio Alba Narrativa, 2014), *Nefando* (Candaya, 2016), and *Mandíbula* (Candaya, 2018; published in English as *Jawbone*, 2022), as well as the poetry collections *El ciclo de las piedras* (Rastro de la Iguana, 2015) and *Historia de la leche* (Candaya, 2020). She has been selected as one of the most relevant literary voices in Latin America by the Hay Festival's Bogotá39 2017 and the 2021 *Granta en Español* list of Best Young Spanish Language Novelists. She received the Prince Claus Next Generation Award in honor of her outstanding literary achievements in 2019; in 2022, she was a National Book Award finalist for the English translation of *Jawbone*.

Sarah Booker is an educator and literary translator working from Spanish to English. Her translations include Mónica Ojeda's *Jawbone* (Coffee House Press, 2022; National Book Award Finalist), Gabriela Ponce's *Blood Red* (Restless Books, 2022), and Cristina Rivera Garza's *New and Selected Stories* (Dorothy Press, 2022), *Grieving: Dispatches from a Wounded Country* (Feminist Press, 2020), and *The Iliac Crest* (Feminist Press, 2017; And Other Stories, 2018). She has a PhD in Hispanic literature from the University of North Carolina at Chapel Hill, and is currently based in Morganton, North Carolina.

Nefando was designed by
Bookmobile Design & Digital Publisher Services.
Text is set in Minion Pro.